MAPLE SUGAR CRUSH

BETH LABONTE

Last Thanksgiving

"I'm just so excited about the inn!" I said, scooping mashed potatoes onto my plate and passing the bowl along to my sister. "I have so many ideas! I'm thinking wind spinners for the front lawn! They have some amazing ones on QVC right now, so I went ahead and ordered ten. If Kit and Amy don't want them, I'll just donate them, well…somewhere! The funeral home could always use some brightening up! Oh, and you should really see the drawings that Kit's mother did in her journal. They're *so* gorgeous. Amy is so lucky she gets to work there—part-time, of course, since she's still writing her books. She's the *best* author. I'm hoping they let me work there too, even though I'm already so busy at Pumpkin Everything, and—"

I looked across the table at my mother, whose face had frozen into a semi-interested half-smile. I do tend to ramble. Or perhaps she'd gone in for a bit of pre-Thanksgiving Botox.

"Sorry." I shrugged. "It's just been a long time since I've had something to look forward to."

"What I don't understand, is why do you still want to work at all?" asked Mom. "All this talk about working at the inn, working at the store. Why not just relax? You could be living down here with us, by the ocean, where it doesn't always smell like pumpkins and manure. You could buy a yacht!"

"Autumnboro doesn't smell like manure, Mom. And you know I'm not crazy about boats. Way too many ways to drown. Besides, I'm only thirty. I'd go out of my mind if I retired now."

I glanced across the table at my father, because even in his fifties I knew he probably felt the same way. I often thought he'd have been happier had I never won all this money. All this money being the $458,000,000 Powerball jackpot I'd hit five years ago. I know, right? Go ahead and pick yourself up off the floor. I sure had to when *I* found out.

"I'm happy for you, Josie," said my sister Meg, giving my hand a squeeze. "It's nice that you've made a home for yourself in Autumnboro. And found such good friends."

"Yeah, it must be *so* tough being a multi-millionaire," said my cousin Audrey, glopping a spoonful of potatoes onto her plate. "I feel *so* bad for you." She passed the bowl to her husband Randy, who snorted in agreement.

"Tell us, Josie," said my uncle Burt, from the other end of the table, "have you booked a seat on that spaceship to Mars yet?" He let out a loud guffaw, clearly pleased with his cleverness. He made that same joke every time he saw me.

"Not yet," I said, rolling my eyes and taking a sip of wine. "But I'm happy to pay for your trip, Uncle Burt. I hear it's a one-way."

"You'd better take her up on that," said my aunt Carla, pointing a fork in her husband's direction. "That's the most generous she's been with any of us."

"That is *not* true!" said Dad, his own fork clattering to his plate as he glared down the table at his sister. "Josie has been very generous with all of us! It's not her fault if you people don't know how to manage your finances." He loosened his collar and went back to eating.

This was typical.

I'd already spent the greater part of the day dodging requests for money. Everywhere I turned, another relation seemed to pop out of the woodwork with their hand out. Not to be one of those *winning the lottery ruined my life* types, but family get-togethers have become a major source of anxiety. It's just a fact. My money, and what I've been doing with it, is pretty much all we ever talk about. They think I'm wasting it. The funny thing is that I mostly try to do *good* things with my money, rather than blowing it on the frivolous materialistic sort of junk they would choose.

After I'd won, I'd taken care of my immediate family first. I bought Meg and her husband Dave a nice house in Kennebunkport, and set up college funds for my two nieces. Then I made sure they quit their jobs and pursued their dream of opening up a coffee shop, which they'd kindly named Josie Beans.

I bought my parents and my grandmother an oceanfront home on Cape Cod—where we were now enjoying Thanksgiving dinner—and pushed them into a relatively early retirement. Mom quit her office manager job of thirty years, and gleefully leaped into a life of leisure. She made friends with all the neighborhood ladies, took up golf, and sought out every anti-aging potion money could buy. I'd introduced her to QVC—along with the fact that Amy's mother was a host—which may have been a mistake, but there was no stopping her now. Dad, who maybe hadn't been quite ready to retire from teaching, seemed bored. He wasn't interested in shopping or golf. He'd taken to walking up and down the beach with a beat-up metal detector he'd found at a local flea market. Granny lives in the in-law apartment and has been having trouble with her memory these past few years. Having her around to care for might be the only thing still grounding my mother to reality.

As for the extended family, I'd followed the advice of my financial planner by paying off their debts and gifting them with enough money that—had they invested it wisely—would have taken care of them for life. I looked over at Uncle Burt, who was picking his teeth with the wishbone. Not all of them had been so wise.

"She could always be slightly *more* generous, couldn't she?" asked Audrey. "It's not like she's in danger of ever running out of money."

"How much did you win, dear?" asked Granny, leaning forward with interest, as if I'd hit twenty bucks on a scratch ticket. No matter how much the family went on about it, Granny never managed to remember. The one time I refreshed her memory, she had to be taken to the emergency room with heart palpitations, so I've been playing it down ever since.

"That's not important, Granny. More wine?" I refilled her glass with cranberry juice.

"What are you down to now?" asked Audrey. "Four hundred and fifty-seven mil?" Granny's eyes widened and she clutched at her necklace.

"She's *joking*," I said, shooting Audrey a look. "Weren't you?"

"Of course," said Audrey, giving Granny a patronizing smile. "I was totally kidding. It's all one…big…funny…joke." She eyed me as she annunciated the last four words.

"What do you even do with it, anyway?" asked Randy. "You don't travel, you don't have a boyfriend…" He ticked each item off on his beefy fingers. As if *he* had any right to comment on my love life. Audrey's no peach, but how he even ended up with *her* is beyond me.

"I donate to countless charities," I said, placing one hand on my chest. "I just invested in my friend's inn! Haven't you been listening at all?"

"And here *we* are, struggling to pay for groceries each week," said Audrey, shaking her head and looking around the table for sympathy.

"I have five dollars in my purse, dear," said Granny, rewarding her with an understanding frown. "I'll give it to you after dinner. But you have to promise to split it with your brother."

"Granny, keep your money." I turned back to Audrey and Randy. "I gave you two *plenty*," I hissed, out of Granny's range of hearing. "How can you possibly not be able to pay for *groceries?*"

"Speaking of being thirty, Josie," interrupted Mom, apropos of nothing. "Have you met any men up there in New Hampshire?" She talked about New Hampshire as if it were a faraway land, even though we'd lived there most of our lives. It was only two years ago that my parents moved from Nashua to Cape Cod, and I decided to start over fresh in Autumnboro.

"Of course, I've met some *men*," I said, grateful for the change of subject. Even if the subject was still me, at least we weren't talking about my money. "There's Kit and Riley. Moose and Donnie. And Tom, of course. He's the best."

"Oh," said Mom, her face lighting up. She gripped the edge of the table with perfectly polished, burgundy nails. "Who's this Tom?"

"Amy's grandpa. He owns Pumpkin Everything, remember? Drove his Jeep through the front of Dunkin Donuts? That's why Amy had to come home in the first place, to make sure he didn't get moved into assisted living and—"

"Never mind," groaned Mom, resting her forehead in her palm and holding the other hand up in the air. "I remember. For a minute I thought maybe Tom was *your* age."

"I wish. He has a girlfriend, anyway. Maggie. She used to be married to Peter Hays, who co-owned the funeral home. She still works there part-time."

"Of course, she does," mumbled Mom, running her fingers through her dyed blonde bob. "Meg, the wine please." My sister passed her the bottle and Mom refilled her glass.

"The turkey was delicious, by the way," said Dad. "You did a wonderful job, Josie. As usual."

"Hear, hear!" said Meg, clinking my wine glass.

"The Winchesters hired a chef this year, did I tell you?" said Mom. "Michelin starred."

"Which means they cooked up some sort of frou-frou tofurkey nonsense," said Dad. "I'll take Josie's regular cooking any day. She's *dad*-starred."

"Thanks, Dad" I said, blinking back a few tears. His jokes were lame, but sweet. Exactly what you needed from a dad on Thanksgiving.

The first Thanksgiving after I'd won the lottery, Mom wanted to hire a professional chef to cook us dinner. I was so uncomfortable with the thought of us lounging around like kings, waiting to be served, that I told Mom if she didn't want to cook anymore, I'd be happy to do it. She didn't put up much of a fight, and I've been doing it ever since.

Once dinner was over, I went into the kitchen to put on a pot of coffee and prepare for dessert. I may have gone a little overboard with the desserts. I've always liked to support Autumnboro's small businesses, so this year I ordered pies from both The Plaid Apple and The Shaky Maple. But then, some high school kids stopped by the store selling pies to support the marching band, so I'd ordered a few from them, as well. Then some *more* kids had come by, selling pies to support the football team, and when I tried to tell them I'd already ordered from the marching band, they looked seriously offended and said, "We have literally nothing to do with each other," and also, "Didn't you win the lottery?" So, I ordered five more.

Then there was the flyer somebody left in my mailbox, saying that Grayson's Turkey Farm was donating half of their Thanksgiving pie proceeds to the animal shelter, so I went ahead and ordered twenty from them. *Twenty.* I know. I ended up giving some away around town, and I left a few in the freezer at home, but even so…it's a good thing Mom and Dad's new house came with a big refrigerator.

I was half inside said refrigerator, trying to extricate the pie boxes, when the doorbell rang.

"Josie!" called Mom. "Could you come out here, please?"

I took a step back, closed the refrigerator doors, and took a deep breath. Some distant relative must have decided to stop by to beg me for money. This was nothing new, but I still hated it. I walked toward the living room, my palms starting to sweat as I rehearsed in my head how I was going to tactfully say no. Maybe if things hadn't gone so wrong for me so early on, I'd still be handing out cash left and right. But people lie, and people take advantage, and I've learned the hard way that sometimes I just have to say no.

I walked into the living room to find Mom standing in front of the couch surrounded by three floppy-haired men. They were all various shades of blond and tan, dressed in khaki pants and identical black peacoats.

"Josie, this is Quinn, Dylan, and Brady. They've come by for dessert!"

"Oh," I said, nodding around at the three of them. "Hello. Are we… related?" I glanced at Mom for assistance. I'd never heard of there being a Quinn, Dylan, or Brady in the family, but you never did know. Like I said, they popped out of the woodwork.

Mom laughed and ran her fingers through her hair. "I certainly hope not! Boys, introduce yourselves!"

"Hey there," said Quinn, shrugging out of his coat and tossing it onto the couch. "I teach golf lessons at the club. Shelly's a real natural." He gave my mother a wink as he mimed a golf swing.

"I clean your parents' pool in the summer," said Dylan, attempting to follow Quinn's lead by miming a pool vacuum, which didn't look nearly as cool as he'd probably hoped. He tossed his coat on top of Quinn's.

Brady gave me a small wave. He seemed a bit shy. Almost as if Mom had thrown him into a sack and kidnapped him from his Thanksgiving dinner, which wasn't out of the question. She'd had a lot of free time while I was busy cooking. "I shampoo at your mom's salon."

"Very nice," I said, nodding politely as understanding sank in.

"Would you three excuse us a minute?" I grabbed my mother by the elbow and marched her back into the kitchen.

"Aren't they just adorable?" she asked.

"How much have you told them about me?"

"What do you mean?"

"I mean, have you told them that I won the lottery?"

"Of course, I did. Everybody around here knows that. They certainly don't think a retired teacher and an office manager could afford a place like this!" She laughed as she leaned back against the island, sliding her hands across the granite.

"Mom," I sighed. "I've told you this before. Dating in my situation is extremely complicated. Have you already forgotten about Dean?" Just saying his name made my stomach turn over.

"Oh, please. These boys are nothing like Dean. You met Dean *online*."

"Who'd she meet online?" asked Uncle Burt, suddenly appearing in the kitchen. He whistled when he saw the stack of pie boxes, then walked to the refrigerator and helped himself to another beer. "One of those Nigerian princes? I bet she'd give a boatload of money to *him* if he asked."

"Maybe if he asked me *nicely*," I said, turning back to my mother. "Look, it doesn't matter *where* I meet them, Mom. There are two things that I know about men: if they're not after my money from the very beginning, they're going to be after it eventually. And it doesn't help when you've gone and filled them in on all the details before they've even met me." I motioned toward the living room. "Although, Brady does seem sweet."

"Doesn't he? And he has the *gentlest* hands." She practically moaned as she pushed me back toward the door. "Go! Talk to him! He can love you for your personality *and* your money!"

"Mom, *no*," I said, turning back around and planting my feet. "I know you're trying to help, but you don't understand how hard this is. Now, I'm going to set out the desserts, and the guys are welcome to stay since I brought a zillion different pies, but I will *not* be flirting with them or playing any sort of dating games. Do you understand? Promise me that you won't keep on giving them the wrong idea."

"Okay," said Mom, holding her hands in the air. "I promise."

I love my mother, but she didn't keep her promise.

By the end of dessert, she'd talked me and my money up so much that Meg had to take Granny upstairs for a nap, and I found myself declining a dinner invitation, a weekend in Nantucket, and a marriage proposal.

"I'm sorry," I said, as the guys filed glumly past me and down the porch steps. "It's not you, it's me! You all seem very sweet!" Brady was the last one out the door, and I put my hand on his arm to stop him. "By the way, my mother mentioned that she'd like you to be a bit rougher when shampooing her head. Really shake her around, if you could."

As I watched their taillights disappear down the road, I had a brief longing for the way Thanksgiving used to be. Back when I was young enough that my mother wasn't obsessed with finding me a husband, and nobody wanted anything from me other than simply being present at the table. Then a wave of guilt walloped me in the stomach, as it always did when I thought about the possibility of life having been better before I'd won the lottery.

I drove home the next morning, happy to be on my way back to my quiet life in Autumnboro, where I had my job at the store and my upcoming involvement with the inn. My life was full. So what if I didn't have a boyfriend? Nobody was meant to have it all. I'd already won Powerball, which made me luckier than nearly everybody else on Earth. It was a one in three hundred million chance.

How dare I expect anything more?

CHAPTER 1

"*D*o you know how many people in this town have no place to go for Thanksgiving?" I asked, looking over the top of the newspaper. It was the week after Halloween, and things were pretty quiet at Pumpkin Everything. Most of the tourists were gone, though they'd be back soon enough for ski season. Tom was dusting shelves while I sat behind the counter reading a copy of *The Autumnboro Times.* My dog, Pixie, sat on the floor by my feet.

"How many?" he asked.

"A lot," I said, looking back down at the troubling statistics. "Too many. I mean, everybody should have *somewhere* to go, don't you think?"

The newspaper had taken a poll, and it broke my heart seeing how many people in our little town had spent Thanksgiving alone last year. Widows and widowers. Families going through divorces. People who simply couldn't afford to travel. While I'd been on the Cape—arguing with my relatives and fending off the advances of the floppy-haired trio—these people had been all by themselves. To me, being alone seemed like the worst fate in the world. I *loved* being around people, which made the fact that most of them only wanted to be friends with me because of my money even harder to bear. It made my real friends like Tom, Kit, and Amy all the more special.

Unfortunately, the newspaper wasn't offering any suggestions on how to help. They'd just printed a photograph of an old woman sitting alone on a bench, holding a pie in her lap. I squinted as I looked more closely at the photo. The letters *H-I-N-G* were on the front of the building behind her. Did they take that right outside my store? How had I missed a lonely old lady sitting out there with a pie in her lap? I frowned, absently scratching Pixie on the head; standing on her hind legs, her chin just barely reached my lap.

I put the newspaper down and walked over to the stack of boxes that had just been delivered, Pixie following me. After Tom sold me Pumpkin Everything earlier this year, I made the decision to start stocking a few Christmas items. Tom assured me that his late wife, Lillian, was rolling over in her grave—she'd named the place *Pumpkin Everything* for a reason, didn't I know? —but eventually agreed that maybe it was a good idea. Since I hadn't lived my entire life in Autumnboro, I didn't have quite the same obsession with fall that everybody else around here did. I mean, I liked it well enough; I can't imagine there's anybody out there who *hates* fall foliage. Amy did hate the smell of pumpkin spice for a while, but that's a whole other story. Anyway, I just happened to like Christmas a lot, too. Why not branch out?

"You'll be going to the Cape for Thanksgiving again, I assume?" asked Tom.

"Actually, I'm not going this year," I said, pulling out a reindeer oven mitt and gently nipping him on the shoulder.

"What do you mean?" asked Tom, batting away the mitt, his puffy white eyebrows furrowed in concern. "How come?"

"Well, last year was a bit...stressful." I dug further into the box, uncovering bags of Christmas-flavored coffees with whimsical names. Tom was going to kill me. "I told you about my aunt and uncle, and my cousin, and my mother the matchmaker, right? I just thought I'd take a little break from all the stressful family drama."

After last Thanksgiving, I'd caved in and written all of them more checks. Audrey and Randy went straight out and bought an RV, which they'd used to take Uncle Burt and Aunt Carla on a month-long tour of America's greatest casinos. I don't need to tell you how that adventure ended. And then, a few weeks ago, I got an email from some distant relative who'd run into my parents at a funeral, finagled an invitation to this year's Thanksgiving dinner, and had just the most incredible idea for a business if only they had the money to get started. They couldn't *wait* to meet me. I just didn't think I could face it. Never mind my mother, who would have a new lineup of gold-digging bachelors waiting, despite everything I had said. Despite everything that had made me believe dating simply wasn't in the cards for me.

"I didn't realize you weren't going home," said Tom, "or I never would have—" He paused when he noticed the bags of coffee. His eyes narrowed. *"Jingle Bell Spice?* What does that even mean?"

"Don't worry about it." I plucked the bag out of his hands. "You would never have what? What are you guys doing for Thanksgiving? Sharyn's coming up, right?"

The idea of staying in Autumnboro and spending Thanksgiving with Tom and his family had definitely crossed my mind. I imagined us testing out the new kitchen at The Autumnboro Inn, and eating a cozy dinner in the dining room by the fireplace. With the inn nearly ready to open, the timing for a test run would be perfect. I may have planned out a menu.

"Well, that's the thing," said Tom, avoiding my eyes. "I was planning to ask you for some time off. It was sort of a last-minute decision, but Amy, Kit, and I, we're going down to Pennsylvania for a couple of weeks. Maggie's coming, too. The inn is pretty much finished, and with it opening next month, this is the last chance they'll have to get away. I hate to leave you in the lurch like this. But like I said, it was a last-minute decision."

My heart sank as my idea of Thanksgiving at the inn went up in smoke. While I loved having Tom around at the store, I certainly wasn't going to crash and burn without him. But that didn't mean I wasn't going to miss him. I'd miss all of them. A couple of weeks without my friends was a very long time.

"Don't be silly!" I said, pasting a bright smile on my face. "Lord knows those two deserve a break, and you deserve to spend some time with your daughter. I'm happy for you!" I turned around and busied myself with pulling bags of coffee out of the box and stacking them into a nearby hutch.

"We assumed you were going to the Cape, darling," said Tom softly. "Otherwise, we would have invited you along. You know you're like family to us. Let me call Amy! Maybe we can still book you on the plane."

"Oh, please," I said, glancing at him over my shoulder. "You know I don't fly. And if I did, I'd rent a private plane. But I'll be fine here. Someone has to keep the store open."

"Are you sure?"

"Absolutely," I said. "Maybe I'll even open for Black Friday!"

That did sound sort of exciting. I could do some major mark-downs and clear out some of the fall stuff that nobody wanted— Rotten Pumpkin scented candles made a great gag gift, but we'd never sold more than three of those things. Then there was the carton of pumpkin spice-flavored Tums that Tom thought would be a real hit with the senior citizens. It was not.

I walked back over to the counter and looked again at the newspaper photo of the old lady with the pie. So, what *was* I going to do for Thanksgiving? I'd been stupidly counting on spending it with Tom and his family. I still didn't want to face the drama of going to the Cape, but I didn't want to spend the day alone, either. The thought of that made my stomach sink. I could invite Meg and her family down to my house, but it wasn't fair to expect them to give up Thanksgiving with the rest of the family. As I looked at the photo, an idea came to me.

"Hey, Tom?" I said.

"Yes, darling?"

"I have an idea."

"It's not about goat yoga again, is it?"

"No, it's not about *goat yoga*," I said, shooting him a look. "It's about Thanksgiving. What if I host a dinner for all the people who don't have a place to go?" I turned around and held up the newspaper. Tom came over and took it out of my hand.

"I think you're a lovely, generous young lady," he said. "And if anybody can pull it off, it would be you. But just so you know, that's Margie Warton in that photo. She has thirteen grandchildren and has been shacking up with Walter Packard for sixteen years. She must've been waiting for the senior shuttle to come by when they took that picture. She always brings a pie to our potluck." He held one hand up to the side of his mouth. "Not homemade."

"Oh," I said, trying to look at the photo from a different perspective. "Okay, well, that's a good thing! I'm glad she's not lonely. But there are still plenty of people who are, and I could make a real difference. I could put an ad in the newspaper! Then there's the food. How many turkeys do you think I'd need? Fifteen? Twenty? How does one go about cooking twenty turkeys? I might need to order a few ovens..."

Tom just shook his head and grabbed his coat. "I'm going across the street for coffee, would you like anything?"

"Sure," I said. "One more PSL before they go out of style. Take this." I pulled a ten-dollar bill out of my wallet.

Tom waved it away. "It's on me today. Let an old man feel useful."

"Fine. But I'm buying you an extra pair of socks this Christmas. Cashmere. No, wait! Alpaca!"

"Lovely."

As soon as he left, I opened my laptop and began making a list of ideas. I had visions of a huge hall lit by candles and white fairy lights, with long tables covered in cornucopias and mountains of food. The more I envisioned it, the more it morphed into the Great Hall at Hogwarts, with candles floating above the tables and owls swooping around. It was a shame a place like that didn't really exist, since I actually had the means to rent it out and fill it with owls. But that was okay. Since I was trying to *avoid* stress and drama on Thanksgiving, I should probably try to keep this thing relatively small. I'd find a suitable location right here in town. Sourcing everything locally would be another way of giving back to the community.

Why hadn't I thought of doing this sort of thing before? I brought free food and coffee to the people who worked around Main Street, I donated to animal shelters and hospitals, I purchased mosquito nets for children in Africa, and I sent two students from Autumnboro High School to college each year on scholarships. But I'd never considered doing something like this, which meant there were countless other things I hadn't thought of, either. Guilt settled in my stomach, as it always did when I thought about how I wasn't doing nearly as much as I could. *One good deed at a time,* I told myself, taking a deep breath. Those were my dad's words. I did feel bad about not seeing my dad for Thanksgiving this year, but I'd go down for a visit soon after. It would be easier without the extended family around, and Mom would hopefully be too distracted by Christmas shopping and yacht club holiday galas to worry about my love life.

I looked across the store and noticed that Tom had left his cardigan draped over the back of a chair. Before he returned with our coffee, I walked over and slipped a ten-dollar bill into the pocket.

CHAPTER 2

"It all just looks so beautiful," I said, my eyes tearing up as I looked around the lobby of The Autumnboro Inn. The old two-family Victorian home that Kit and Amy had grown up in had undergone an incredible transformation over the past year. I was so happy that my money had been able to help make Rebecca Parker's dream a reality, I got teary-eyed every single time I came by. Not helping my emotional state, were the colored pencil drawings from her journal that Kit had framed and hung in various places around the inn. I walked over to the one by the coat rack, then looked past it into the living room. It was almost a perfect recreation.

"Is there anything I can do?" I asked, following Amy into the living room. My heart lifted when I saw the Christmas tree standing in the front window, then sank a bit when I realized it had already been decorated with silver and white pumpkin ornaments. A scarecrow was perched on top, where the angel would normally be. With its mid-December grand opening, the inn was an interesting mix of both autumn and Christmas décor.

When I'd first offered to invest in the inn, I'd had so many grand ideas of how I would be involved in the decorating, the advertising, the day-to-day inner workings. I saw now that I was just a tad bit overexcited, bordering on delusional. I was a silent partner which, according to the internet, means *an individual whose partnership is limited to providing capital to the business*. Being a silent partner does not include purchasing six Catherine Zeta-Jones Sherpa blankets without the consent of the general partner. Live and learn. Still, it was sort of a bummer.

"You're our sole investor, Josie," said Amy. "Believe me, you've already done more than enough."

"I know *that*," I said, glancing around the rest of the room. There seemed to already be an autumn decoration on every available surface, and a pile of Sherpa blankets in a basket by the couch. Darn it. Even the glass case protecting Tom's model stage-coach had been outlined in orange and white lights. I stepped over the electrical cord that was running across the room (total trip hazard if you asked me—which they hadn't), and craned my neck toward the kitchen. "I wasn't talking about money. I was thinking more along the lines of decorating, or maybe helping to check in guests, or...oh! I could carry their luggage up the stairs! Don't you think it would be fun to be a bellhop?" I gazed at the main staircase, imagining myself in a cute uniform with a little hat, effortlessly heaving suitcases up the steps.

"Um, maybe?" said Amy, giving me the same exact look that Tom had when I'd mentioned goat yoga. It was uncanny. "Only, Kit's planning on doing all the check-ins and helping guests with their luggage. We only have six rooms, so it shouldn't be a big deal. And we've been working our butts off to get all the deco-rating done in time. I still can't believe we're opening in just a few weeks!" She looked at me with a wide-eyed, exaggerated expression of excitement and fear.

"Oh, you'll be fine!" I said, pulling her into a hug. "It's going to be great! I'm so proud of you two."

I really was. During the chaos of renovations, Kit and Amy had also managed to squeeze in a wedding and a honeymoon. To be honest, the way those two had reunited after ten years apart, the entire past year seemed like a honeymoon for them. Most of it, at least. There was a brief time—after Amy first found out that Kit wanted to remodel their childhood home into an inn, forcing Tom to move out—when I wasn't sure if they were going to be able to make things work. But once Tom gave Amy his blessing to let go of the house, everything worked out like a dream.

Which leads me to another reason I hadn't been as involved with the inn as I'd hoped. As soon as renovations had gotten underway, I realized that I was nothing but a big, fat third wheel. Between Kit and Amy's PDAs and the playful butt smacking, it didn't take me long to vacate the premises.

"Thanks," said Amy, hugging me back. "Do you find it at all strange, though, having an autumn-themed inn around Christmastime?" She glanced nervously at the tree.

"You realize you live in an autumn-themed town year-round, right?" asked Kit, appearing on the stairs in a hooded sweatshirt and jeans. When he got to the bottom, he planted a kiss on top of his wife's head.

"Of *course*, I do," said Amy, slipping her arm around his waist. "I'm just saying that it seems even stranger when you see it all thrown together in one tiny place."

"And you're telling me this now?"

"I'm sorry! Forget I said anything!"

"Now it's all I can see," said Kit, nervously surveying the room, his eyes landing on the scarecrow atop the Christmas tree. "I know that Josie cries every time she sets foot in here, but I always assumed that was a good thing."

"It is!" I said. "The place looks amazing, guys. Don't change a thing. So, are you all pa—"

I was about to ask if they were all packed for their trip to Pennsylvania, when Amy smacked Kit on the butt and the two of them took off giggling into the kitchen, leaving me alone in the living room. Right. Maybe I should add *invisible* to my title. Josie Morgan, Invisible Silent Partner.

I felt a small pang of jealousy, as I heard more laughter coming from the kitchen. The fact that I could be jealous of anybody was a laugh in itself, but there it was. Sometimes I liked to ponder the idea of "giving it all up" for love. Like, if a big blue genie appeared and made me an offer, would I take it? The fact that I didn't one hundred percent know my answer always left me feeling ungrateful. There were people who would kill to be in my situation. How dare I have the nerve to go around dreaming about giving it all up for some hot guy?

Not that he'd need to be *hot*, per se. Just sweet, and kind, and open to the idea of owning a capuchin monkey (though totally not a deal breaker). The best part is that I wouldn't have to worry about him using me for my money, because the money would be gone! I'd have given it all up for love, which would either be incredibly stupid or incredibly romantic. Either way, the whole fantasy seemed so anti-girl-power that I didn't dare mention a word of it to anyone but Pixie.

When Kit and Amy still hadn't returned after several minutes, I decided I should probably get going. I grabbed my purse just as the front door opened, and in walked Kit's younger brother, Riley. A few butterflies, who clearly didn't understand *anything*, stirred in my stomach.

"Hey, Moneybags," said Riley, tossing a big, brown jacket onto the reception desk and knocking over a pencil cup. "Kit left this at my apartment yesterday. Is he around?"

I jerked my head toward the kitchen, where the sound of Amy's laughter was followed by a disturbing sort of a slurp. I really hoped that was the coffeemaker.

"Gross," said Riley.

"Tell me about it. I thought that sort of thing would have worn off by now. But, what do I know?"

Riley walked past me into the sitting area and flopped down

on the couch. He put his feet up on the coffee table. It was a weekday, so he was dressed in his funeral home work clothes—dark gray suit, white shirt, black tie. He'd been letting his facial hair grow a bit since the summer, and his dark hair looked freshly cut—short on the sides, with the longer top part combed over. No, not like a *combover*. Like…modern. Cute.

Last fall, I ended up as part of a group Halloween costume with Riley, Tom, and Maggie. We'd all dressed up as Pokémon characters, and the whole night had been so much fun. It all started with Amy surprising Kit with the deed to her grandfather's house, followed by handing out candy to trick-or-treaters at Pumpkin Everything, followed by a late-night party back at Kit and Riley's apartment. I'd known Riley for a while at that point, never thinking of him as anything other than a friend. But after a few pumpkin ales, I'd found myself strangely attracted to the way he popped bite-sized Snickers into his mouth—one after the other—while slumped all casual-like on the couch, staring at his phone. Normally, a grown man in a Pikachu costume would be nothing to get worked up about. But that night…

Anyway, I'd kept one eye on him over the winter, but it wasn't until this past summer that I may have gone and developed a teensy little crush. With Kit and Amy all wrapped up in each other and their wedding plans, Riley had seemed a little lonely. I'd felt bad that he'd been forced to move out of the house he'd grown up in and into his own apartment all the way over in Summerboro. I'd been feeling lonely, too, with Amy so preoccupied, and even Tom spending more and more time with Maggie. Pixie and I had started stopping by the funeral home every so often with a frozen Maple Sugar Crush, which I'd found out from the barista at The Shaky Maple was Riley's favorite drink. I'd slipped her a twenty for her trouble.

I tried to make small talk about things I thought he'd be interested in—tombstone engravings, the outrageous cost of floral arrangements—but he was never very chatty. He was always busy with meetings, and paperwork, and sometimes he'd even disappear down to the casket showroom where, believe me, I wasn't ever setting foot. Usually I'd end up back at the reception desk, chatting with Maggie or Artie Goldwyn. Those two *loved* to talk about tombstone engravings and the outrageous cost of floral arrangements.

But one day, as Riley was passing the reception desk on his way out for a lunchtime walk, he invited me along. He'd seemed nervous, and the invitation had taken me completely by surprise. We ended up playing Pokémon Go all over town. As we walked, I rambled away about my life, and he offered up some behind-the-scenes stories from his job (which led to more than a few sleepless nights, and not in a good way). After that, I started doubling the amount of time I spent at the funeral home, and we went on more and more walks, and that's when the butterflies started.

I puttered around by the entrance to the inn, delaying my decision to leave, while Riley took out his phone. I watched his dark brown eyes dart around the screen, wondering, for a moment, not what life would have been like had I never won the lottery, but what life would have been like had smartphones never been invented. As if he'd read my mind, Riley suddenly looked straight at me.

"What?" I asked, my cheeks warming. Was there something stuck to my face? I swiped at my chin. "What is it?"

"There's an Aerodactyl on your head. Hold very, very still." He held up his phone and started tapping at the screen.

I sighed, but held still until he'd finished.

"All set. I was just kidding about not moving, by the way."

I rolled my eyes and picked up the stapler, then put it down again. Righted the pencil cup. I wished Kit and Amy would hurry up with whatever they were doing in the kitchen. Hopefully, if they were going to do *it,* they'd at least have had the decency to go upstairs. Since I hadn't seen them sneak out of the kitchen, they were probably just making out. But still. I could always just leave, like I'd planned, but now I felt bad abandoning Riley here by himself. Not that he seemed to care.

"So, are you all packed?" I asked, walking over and sitting down in the chair across from him.

"For what?"

"Pennsylvania? Thanksgiving?"

"Why would I go to Pennsylvania for Thanksgiving?" He jabbed at his phone screen several more times, still not looking up.

I sighed. "I don't know, maybe because Kit's going and you're a member of his family? Or have you gone and married your phone?"

His fingers stopped moving, his eyes finally looking up in my direction. He flipped the phone facedown on his lap. "Sorry. No, I'm not going with them."

"Oh, that's right," I said, suddenly realizing, like a big dope, why he wasn't going. "You're spending the holiday with Catrina's family. Duh."

One day, toward the end of the summer, as I'd been heading to the funeral home with a fresh Maple Sugar Crush and a flock of dim-witted butterflies in my belly, I'd seen Riley already out on the common. He was sitting in a tire swing and drinking a Maple Sugar Crush, alongside Catrina Corman. Catrina's dad owned Corman Memorials over in Summerboro—which worked closely with Goldwyn & Hays—so, those two obviously had a ton in common. Riley was really laughing it up, and his phone wasn't anywhere in sight, which never happened when he was with me. Never mind that stuffy, one-word-answer Riley was sitting *in a freaking tire swing* and smiling about it. But that was fine. I'd started out trying to be his friend, and he clearly hadn't needed one as much as I'd thought. He had Catrina, so he wasn't lonely like I was, and that was a *good* thing.

I'd stopped going by the funeral home after that.

CHAPTER 3

"*C*atrina?" asked Riley.

He looked completely puzzled. Was he for real? Okay, maybe I hadn't exactly seen the two of them together after the tire swing incident, but I'd asked Amy and she'd definitely confirmed they were dating. I'd asked her if Riley was seeing anybody, and she'd said "Of *course* he is," which, now that I think about it, may have been sarcasm.

In the few seconds that it took me to respond, I'd lost him again. He'd flipped his phone over in his lap, and was lovingly stroking the side of it with his thumb.

I watched his fingers for a few seconds, mesmerized, before clearing my throat.

"Never mind," I said. "So, um, why aren't you going to Pennsylvania, then?"

"Work gets busy this time of year." He shrugged. "I couldn't take that much time off. You going to the Cape?"

"No, I'm staying here," I said, shocked that he had actually remembered my usual Thanksgiving plans. "I'm thinking of hosting a meal for all the people who have no place to go. Did you see the article in *The Autumnboro Times*? It was awful."

"Yeah, I don't think anyone on that staff is up for the Pulitzer."

"I didn't mean that it was *written* terribly," I said, although he did have a point. "I meant the subject matter. So many people all alone for the holidays. It's just so sad." I put one hand on my chest, a sudden knot in my throat. "I've decided that if I'm going to choose to avoid my own family on Thanksgiving, I'd like to help those who don't *have* a choice, you know?"

I expected Riley's eyes to have wandered back to his phone at some point during my ramble, but they were still fixed on me. He was leaning forward, his forearms resting on his legs, and studying me with that same sort of perplexed, frozen expression I'd seen from my mother—minus the judgmental bit behind the eyes. There was something else in his eyes, but they were such a deep, intense shade of brown that I'd always found them hard to read. Most of the time they looked right through me. But now… my idiot stomach did a little flip.

"That's really nice of you," he said, his eyebrows knitting together, a small smile forming at the corner of his mouth.

"Thanks." I swallowed as my eyes darted to the Christmas tree, then back to Riley. "You're welcome to come, too, you know? Since you're going to be alone."

My words broke whatever sort of moment we'd been having, and he slumped back into the chair.

"Alone is fine," he said, his eyes back on his phone. "A turkey sandwich alone in my apartment sounds like a dream, actually."

"Really?" I crinkled my nose. That sounded so sad and lonely and close to what I'd be doing if I didn't have this dinner to host. Why would anybody *choose* that? I really didn't understand him at all.

Before he could answer, Kit and Amy reappeared on the main staircase, looking disheveled. That's when I remembered the newly built *back* staircase that led from the kitchen up to the guest rooms. I held back a laugh as Riley looked up at them, his face slowly registering what was happening.

"Riley! Hey!" said Amy. "I didn't know you were coming by."

"Just dropping off Kit's jacket." He tipped his chin toward the reception desk. "Everything okay? You guys seem out of breath."

"Yeah," she said, giving Kit some serious side-eye. His hair looked nothing like it had twenty minutes ago. "We were just doing some last-minute...dusting."

"And that's why I never drop by unannounced," Riley whispered to me, as he stood up to leave. "I'm going to grab a coffee before I head back to work, anybody want anything?"

"No, thanks," said Amy. "We've got some brewing in the kitchen."

"How about you, Moneybags? PSL? Maple Sugar Crush?" He gave me a wink.

"Um, no, thanks," I said, flustered at the mere mention of a Maple Sugar Crush. As if it were *our* coffee or something. Never mind the wink. What in the world was *that* about? After the door closed behind him, I found Amy watching me with a strange smile on her face.

"What?"

"What was that wink all about?"

I shrugged. "I used to bring him a Maple Sugar Crush once in a while, over the summer, while you and Kit were busy with the inn and the wedding and everything."

"Really?" said Amy, her eyebrows shooting up. "How did I not know about this?"

"Because there was nothing to know. I bring people food and coffee all the time. It's what I *do*." I walked into the kitchen, Amy following closely behind.

Even if Riley and Catrina weren't dating, I'd still seen the way he'd looked when he was talking to someone who actually interested him. Someone who wasn't an annoying, overly chatty, little sister type, tagging along on all his lunch breaks.

"Sure, but bringing Deb a bagel at the senior center is slightly different than *Riley*." Amy slid onto a stool at the island. "You deserve to be happy, Josie. You know that, right?"

"I *am* happy," I said, taking the seat across from her. "I'm rolling in money."

"Which doesn't buy happiness. Haven't you heard the old saying?"

"I don't think anybody had four hundred million bucks in the bank when they invented that saying."

Amy laughed. "Maybe not. Riley's cute though, huh?"

I just blinked back at her, trying to retain my poker face as my cheeks warmed. So what if Riley was cute? Lots of guys were cute. Dean had been *really* cute and he'd turned into the biggest buttface of them all.

"When's the last time you had a boyfriend?" she continued, sounding a lot like my mother.

"None of your business." I poured sugar into my coffee and stirred it with a cinnamon stick. There was a mason jar full of them on the center of the island, wrapped in an autumn plaid bow. "Besides, I don't like to talk about it."

"Wow, if *you* don't want to talk about something, it must be really bad."

I stuck out my tongue and we sat in silence for a few moments, sipping our coffee.

"His name was Dean," I mumbled, at last.

"Huh?"

"My last boyfriend. His name was Dean, and I met him online a few months after I won the lottery."

"Oh," said Amy, her face lighting up. "And?"

"And, I didn't even tell him about the money at first. I thought I was being really smart by waiting until we'd been dating for a couple of months before dropping the P-bomb."

"P-bomb?" She crinkled her nose.

"Powerball."

"Ah, right. So…what did he say when he found out?"

"He was shocked, obviously. But he was happy for me, too. He didn't get all weird, or pressure me to spend it on him or anything, either. He was a totally genuine, totally nice guy back then."

Amy nodded. "I feel a *but* coming."

"*But,* after we'd been dating for almost two years, he told me about this great business idea he had." I rolled my eyes. Everyone always had a great business idea. "Some sort of app that was going to be the next big social media thing. We'd already talked about getting married someday, and all the places we'd travel, and where we'd raise our kids. We had this amazing, blessed life planned out where we could do anything we wanted, so of *course* I gave him the money. We were in this for the long haul. If his idea failed, so what? Anyway, the next thing I knew, he'd pocketed the money and taken off to Thailand."

Amy's jaw dropped. "What do you mean, *he'd taken off to Thailand?*"

"I mean, he hopped on a plane and flew to Thailand and I never heard from him again."

"How do you know where he went if you never heard from him again?"

"I hired a private investigator. I just wanted to know where he'd gone off to, so I'd be sure to never go there. Also, so I could get some closure."

I'd gotten closure all right. Closure on my love life. Sometimes I lay awake at night, imagining what my life with Dean would have been like had I never won the lottery. Dean would have stayed the sweet, loving guy he'd been when we'd first met, rather than going all Saruman on me. I liked to imagine what our children would have looked like, or what other countries we might have seen. We'd only made it to one.

"Wow," said Amy, letting out a whistle. "I'm so sorry, Josie. You always seem so positive. I had no idea you'd been hurt like that."

"It's fine," I said, tilting my head back and looking up at the rose gold pots and pans hanging above the island. "I've been blessed beyond my wildest dreams, Amy. Nobody's meant to have it *all*. Well, except for Jensen Ackles' wife."

"But what does that mean, exactly?" asked Amy, her face filling with concern. "You're going to spend your whole life avoiding meeting someone who might make you happy? I mean, what if you bump into a guy at The Shaky Maple and it's like a love at first sight sort of thing? You're just going to turn and run the other way?"

"Do you know how many people are alone in this world?" I asked, wishing I had that article from *The Autumnboro Times* to wave around. "They spend their whole lives trying to meet someone perfect, and they *still* never do. I think it's safe to say that love isn't going to just fall into my lap. And even if it did, how could I trust that it was real?"

Amy looked at me skeptically. "Well, Riley is Kit's *brother*. You could trust that he'd never take off to Thailand, because Kit would straight up murder him."

"Not the most flattering reason for a guy to stick around."

Amy laughed. "I still think you should give him a chance."

"Give who a chance?" asked Kit, walking into the kitchen.

"Grandpa," said Amy. "He wants to take Josie's Tesla for a spin, and I said she should let him."

I laughed, but to be honest, I'd rather let Tom drive my Tesla through the front of another Dunkin Donuts, than ever trust my heart to another man.

CHAPTER 4

⨫

I wanted to place a Thanksgiving dinner invitation in *The Autumnboro Times* as soon as possible; but before I could do that, I needed to figure out a location.

There was my house, of course. It was certainly big enough, with a lovely view of the Pemigewasset, but I wasn't totally comfortable inviting strangers into my home. Most of the people in this town, if they didn't know me personally, at least knew that I was the "big lottery winner." I tried to always see the best in people, but I wasn't naïve. There was also the possibility that only one person would show up, which would be majorly awkward. Especially if they turned out to be a serial killer. Or Riley Parker. No, I needed to hold this dinner in a public, more neutral sort of a place.

I left Tom in charge of the store the next morning, while I set off down Main Street, zipped inside my winter coat. Pixie was wearing her favorite gray and pink Fair Isle sweater. Some people in my position might have a garage full of classic cars, or an armoire packed with expensive jewelry—I have a closet full of custom-made hand-knit dog sweaters. Believe me, Pixie needs them. She's a Dachshund Chihuahua Jack Russell mix who used to live in a shelter in Florida, but was relocated up north after a hurricane. She *hates* the cold, and now that it's November, the cold is no joke. It could snow at any moment.

Unlike Pixie, I'm actually pretty excited for it to snow. I'll let you in on a little secret: After Halloween, Autumnboro gets pretty darn depressing. There, I said it. Don't tell anybody, or they'll run me out of town. But, it's *true*. The colorful leaves are gone from the trees and nearly all the tourists have left. The pumpkins that had been cheerfully decorating the streets have either been carted off to local farms or had their guts strewn across the sidewalks by hungry squirrels. I've spotted more than a few scarecrows stuffed upside down into trash barrels, which is not a dignified way for *anybody* to go. The energy that had been in the air all season very quickly fizzles into a gray, November dullness.

Blah.

It's not the town's fault or anything. It's just the way it is when your town is themed after a particular season, and that particular season comes to an end. It isn't until the first snowfall that some life comes back into Autumnboro. It's not the same flashy, touristy Autumn Capital of the World sort of life that it had before, but it's still a small New England town blanketed by fresh snow, which has a magic all its own.

"Morning, Josie!"

I glanced back to find Jackie from The Plaid Apple, standing on a ladder. She was taking down her Halloween flag and replacing it with a chubby turkey eating a slice of cherry pie. *Gobble 'til We Wobble!* it read above the turkey's head.

"Morning, Jackie!" I called back. "Cute flag! Good morning, Moose!"

I waved cheerfully across the street to Kyle "Moose" Moriarty, standing outside his mini mart. Moose's nickname had the coolest origin story of all time. When he was sixteen, he'd driven straight between the legs of a moose that was crossing

31

the street during his road test with the DMV. Despite my admiration, Moose hated my guts. He'd told Tom a few months ago that winning the lottery really "messed with my head." Tom repeated it to me because he'd thought it was funny, not realizing that making me out to be a ditz was Moose's way of taking me down a peg. This was somewhat hurtful because a) I'd never done anything to him personally, and b) I've always been this way.

I understood that lottery winners could be hard to stomach, and that Moose had never been handed anything in his life, but it still hurt to be talked about behind my back. I've been trying to be extra friendly toward him ever since. He returned my wave with a grunt, loud enough to be heard across the street, turned around, and went back inside the store.

I crossed the street to buy a few coffees at The Shaky Maple, before continuing on my way to the senior center. The senior center had a large enough space to hold a community dinner, and they also had a kitchen, which was a plus. I opened the door to find a Zumba class in full swing at the back of the room. They'd recently remodeled that area into a brightly painted fitness studio. Closer to the door were several tables filled with people playing cards and board games, or doing puzzles. On the other side of the room was a brand-new shuffleboard table, and a wall-mounted television that was muted and set to Fox News.

The place was hopping. I used to volunteer here all the time, before I'd bought Pumpkin Everything. I still left Tom in charge of the store a few times a week so I could stop by. Sometimes I taught a Zumba class, or helped to serve lunch. Sometimes I just sat and chatted with the seniors, letting them reminisce about the good old days. And sometimes, just for fun, I took them for rides down the Kancamagus in my red Tesla Model S. Arnie and Walter were huge fans of Ludicrous Mode, even though I'd promised Officer Heffley, quite a while back, that I wouldn't be using it anymore. Oopsy.

I scanned the room until I found Deb, the director, working on a bulletin board on the back wall.

"Hi, Deb," I said, walking over and holding out one of the coffees I'd bought. "Still doing PSLs?"

"Josie! You know I'm *always* doing PSLs, but you really shouldn't have." She thanked me as she took the coffee out of my hand, her eyes darting around the room as if making sure everything was in tip-top shape. In addition to volunteering, I made an annual donation.

"Everybody seems to be having a good time," I said, giving her a reassuring smile. I wished she'd relax. I wasn't the type to randomly stop in to check up on how my money was being used. I mean, I didn't even complain when they ignored my idea about the goat yoga.

"They really are," said Deb, her face filling with relief. "The shuffleboard table has been a *huge* hit. What brings you by, dear? I didn't have you on the schedule for today."

"I was just wondering if I could borrow the senior center on Thanksgiving? I know you're not open that day, and I need a big space for a community dinner I'm hosting."

"You're such a doll," said Deb, her face crumpling as she clasped one hand to her chest. "That's a wonderful idea, Josie. Really, just the *best* idea. The thing is, I wish you'd asked me a week ago."

"Oh," I said, my heart sinking. "Sorry. I only came up with the idea yesterday. Did somebody beat me to it?" The idea that somebody else might be planning the same sort of event, after reading that article in the newspaper, hadn't even occurred to me.

"Not exactly," she said. "Margie Wharton's reserved it for her family. All five of her kids, plus her thirteen grandchildren are coming for Thanksgiving, which is too many people to fit in Walter's house. You know they've been shacking up for years?"

"I've heard," I said. At least Tom would get a kick out of this.

"You know what?" said Deb, taking a sip of her latte and

looking me over. "Let me give Margie a call. I'll tell her that the space is no longer available. That's the Josie Morgan fitness studio over there. What has Margie ever done for us? Between you and me, I don't even think her pies are homemade." She whipped out her cell phone and started punching in numbers.

"No!" I said, grabbing her arm. "Please don't cancel on Margie. I can find another place."

I could see it now, Margie blabbing to everyone in town about how I'd stolen the senior center out from under her because I was *so rich*. People would roll their eyes. Talk about how I thought I was better than them. Word would get back to Moose, who would just nod smugly, convinced he'd been right about me all along.

Deb stared at me for a moment before reluctantly putting her phone back into her pocket. "Are you sure?"

"Totally."

"I really am sorry," she said. "Is there anything else we can do for you? Would you like to stay for lunch? It's turkey fricassee day! Or maybe some Zumba while you're here? Ladies! Would you like Josie to join you?"

The entire class turned around and enthusiastically waved me over.

"Sure," I said. "Why not?" I was a sucker for those Latin beats. The turkey fricassee was pretty good, too.

CHAPTER 5

An hour later, I was back out on the street, and back to the drawing board regarding where I was going to hold my dinner. My other idea was Grayson's Turkey Farm. I was planning to order the turkeys from them anyway, and I knew they had a function room where they held banquets and small weddings. It wouldn't hurt to ask. I should probably stock up on canned corn and stuff, too, before everything was sold out. I dropped Pixie off at Pumpkin Everything, where she could curl up in front of the fire, then I walked across the street to Moose's Mini Mart. I dialed the number for the turkey farm.

"Grayson's Turkey Farm, Roy speaking."

"Hey, Roy," I said. I waved to a stone-faced Moose, sitting behind the counter, and headed toward canned goods. "I'd like to place an order for some turkeys?"

"You've come to the right place. What can we get for you?"

"I'm going to need a *lot* of them," I said, surveying the shelves. I probably should have gone to a full-sized grocery store, but like I said, I wanted to buy everything locally. Besides, Moose had recently expanded the mini mart into the empty space next door (the White Mountain Reiki Center had not long for this world, although I thought my session was *amazing*).

"A lot as in…how many?"

"Well, that's the thing." I switched the phone to my left ear, and grabbed every can of cranberry sauce Moose had in stock. "I don't know exactly how many people will be coming yet. I'm thinking around…fifty?" That was actually more than I hoped would turn up, but you never knew.

"Fifty," repeated Roy. "Is this a corporate event?"

"Nope." Boy, my basket was heavy. Moose gave me an odd look as I staggered back to the front of the store and dumped all the cans into a shopping cart. "I'm cooking a Thanksgiving dinner for anybody in town that needs a place to go. What do you think?"

"I think that's incredibly kind of you."

"I mean, what do you think about how many turkeys I'll need?"

"Oh, right. Well, we typically advise one pound per person, so for fifty people that would be about five turkeys."

"Five? That's it?" That couldn't be right. I crinkled my nose and swept Moose's entire inventory of canned corn into my cart. "Can we make it fifteen, just to be safe?"

"You want fifteen turkeys?"

"What's wrong with that?"

"Do you have enough ovens to cook fifteen turkeys?"

"Okay, fine. Make it five."

I pushed my cart to the end of the canned goods aisle, nearly colliding with a figure in black, darting across in front of me. Riley. As usual, he was looking down at his phone instead of up at where he was going. He put one hand on the front of my cart, glancing up with an annoyed expression on his face. When he realized it was me, his expression softened slightly, and he gave me a small smile before continuing on his way.

I stopped my cart in front of the frozen foods while Roy took down my name and address for delivery of the turkeys.

"Josie!" he said. "I didn't realize I was speaking to *you*. How are you doing? Can I interest you in buying pies again this year?"

"I'm great," I said. "And yes, of course. May as well make it thirty pies this time." That way, anyone who came to dinner could also take home some pie.

Roy whistled. "That's why we love you, Josie."

Surprise, surprise. I'd ordered five turkeys and thirty pies, and Roy suddenly loved me. He wouldn't be the first.

"One more thing," I said, before he hung up. "Is your function room available by any chance on Thanksgiving?"

There was a pause while Roy tapped at his computer keyboard. "No, I'm sorry. Margie Wharton's already booked us."

"Margie Wharton? But she's already booked the senior center for her Thanksgiving dinner. What does she need your place for?"

"After-party."

I let out a loud groan. Riley, who'd joined me in the frozen food section, glanced over.

"I could cancel on her," said Roy. "I mean, you're one of our best customers. Let me send her an email." The keyboard tapping started up again.

"No!" I cried. "Please don't. I'll find another place. Thanks anyway, Roy."

I hung up the phone and turned my cart toward the front of the store. Riley was staring straight ahead into the ice cream freezer, so I continued past him without saying a word.

"Hey," said a voice, after I was halfway down the cereal aisle. "Wait up."

I glanced down to where Riley had grabbed the handle of my shopping cart, his hand right up against my own, and felt a stirring of butterflies.

"Oh, hey," I said, removing my hands from the cart and

shoving them into my pockets. I took a step back. He really was quite tall, when he was standing so close. And the mini mart, despite its recent expansion, still lived up to its name when it came to aisle width. I'd backed all the way up against the Cheerios, and we were still only a few feet apart. The collar of his white shirt was undone, his tie loosened. I swallowed. "I didn't know if there was a Squirtle or something in that freezer, so, you know…I didn't want to interrupt. Word to the wise, though, Moose will kill you if you keep those freezer doors open too long."

Riley held up a box of orange Creamsicles. "Believe it or not, I was just getting dessert for the office. Maggie was craving these things. I think they're from her childhood or something."

"The Maple Sugar Crush of her generation." I nodded. "Have you had one today?"

"Nah. Too many of those things will kill you. Or maybe that was part of your plan last summer." His teasing smile, and his second mention of this past summer, made my knees go weak. I reached one hand back, steadying myself against the Rice Krispies and Cocoa Puffs.

"I should let you get those back to the office before they melt," I said, grabbing my cart and continuing on my way. "See you later, Riley."

"Hang on," he said, stopping me again. This time he put his hand completely over mine, sending a jolt of electricity through my body that, with any luck, fried those annoying butterflies to a crisp. "I couldn't help overhearing your phone call. You're still looking for a place to hold that dinner?"

I nodded. "Apparently Margie Wharton's got this whole town in her pocket."

"What about the church?" asked Riley. "Isn't that where those types of things are usually held?"

"Usually," I said. "But I wouldn't even know who to ask over there. Do you?"

"I work at the funeral home," he said. "I have connections."

"Like with—?" My eyes widened as I pointed upward.

"Hopefully," said Riley. "But I don't think we need to go straight to the top in this case."

We continued walking together to the front of the store, where Riley paid Moose for the popsicles, and then pulled out his phone.

"Let me call Susan Blake. When she's not driving the senior shuttle, she's in charge of church social events."

"Okay, thanks," I said, furrowing my brow, still confused as to why Riley was suddenly being so friendly, while also trying my hardest to think of him as a brother or a cousin or a high school gym teacher. *Anything* to keep my hormones under control. Having a crush, when I wasn't interested in dating—or having a fling with somebody I'd have to see on a daily basis after it ended —was completely pointless. I milled around by the newspaper racks while Riley made his phone call. A few minutes later, he was back.

"The church basement is all yours," he said. "Susan said you can use the kitchen, too, so you'll be able to cook at least one of your many turkeys there."

"Thank you!" I said. "That's a really big help. One less thing to worry about. You know, you're still welcome to come. I know you said you didn't want to, but nobody should be alo—"

"Nah," he said, cutting me off. "I'm good. I'll see you later." He gave me a crooked smile and a quick wave as he took off out of the store.

"What are you even doing here?" asked Moose. "Shouldn't you be shopping at ritzy places? Like, Nieman Marcus?"

I peeled my eyes away from Riley's retreating backside, to look at Moose. He was squinting at me and sipping from the big, black tumbler that he always carried around.

"You want me to shop for cranberry sauce at Nieman Marcus?" I pushed my cart over to the register.

Moose just shrugged and began ringing up my things. I sort of hated how much I wanted Moose to like me. It shouldn't matter what he thought of me, as I hadn't done a single thing to offend him personally. He certainly never turned down one of my free coffees. When Amy had come back to Autumnboro last fall, *everybody* was mad at her over the books she'd written, and she ended up having to give an apology speech to the entire town. Was that what I needed to do? Apologize for winning the lottery? That didn't seem fair. Sure, I'd bought the ticket. But I'd never meant to win. I don't think anybody ever *means* to win.

"So, Moose…do you have any job openings?" I asked, already knowing the answer.

"Who's asking?"

"Me," I said, batting my eyelashes.

Moose shook his head, keeping his eyes fixed on the cans he was ringing up. "What'd you do, forget that you're a millionaire?"

"*No.*"

"Did you forget that you already work all day at that store you bought?"

"Nope! I know *both* of those things. But, see, my store closes at five o'clock and yours is open til ten. I could work here a few nights a week and give you some time off. You wouldn't even have to pay me!"

"You're nuts," he said matter-of-factly, which was his usual answer.

Okay, fine. At the present moment, Moose still hated me enough to turn down free labor. But *someday* he'd have to soften up and give me a chance. I always thought it would be fun working at a grocery store—using the price gun, beeping things across the scanner, figuring out the best way to fit everything into bags. That was the main reason I asked for a job. The second reason was because between the time my store closed, and the time that I went to sleep, there were a lot of lonely hours to fill.

Winning over Moose was the third reason, but that wasn't going to happen today. There was one more thing I could do, though.

"I'll take two cartons of Marlboros, also," I said. "Please."

Moose raised his eyebrows. "You're a smoker now?"

"Maybe."

"They're bad for your health."

"What do you care?" I held out my hands. He handed me the cartons, containing twenty packs of cigarettes that would go straight into the trash can outside. That didn't matter. What mattered was that they were the most expensive thing in his store.

"That'll be $326.52," said Moose, his eyes lighting up as he read me the total, as I knew they would.

"Have a great day!" I said, pushing my cart toward the exit. When I glanced back, he was smiling.

CHAPTER 6

⚜

"*I*t's nothing personal," I said, flopping back against the couch pillows. I had *Sharyn's Closet* muted on the television, watching as Amy's mother buzzed back and forth between clothing racks. I was on the phone, trying to tactfully explain to my own mother, for the millionth time, why I wasn't coming home this year for Thanksgiving. "I just feel like hosting this community dinner is something I need to do. These people really need me."

"But what will everyone *think*?" asked Mom, also for the millionth time. By *everyone*, she meant her friends and neighbors on the Cape.

"I don't know, maybe that you raised me to be a kind and empathetic human being?" I said. "It's not like I'm not coming because I'm stuck in jail or something."

I pictured her standing at the kitchen window, looking out at the ocean and fretting over this bit of news that was probably the worst thing to happen to her in quite some time. She'd been living a charmed life since I'd won the lottery. Not getting her way for once might actually be good for her.

"*Maybe*," said Mom, skeptically. "But it's not just that, Josie.

I've already made some…arrangements. Arrangements that will be very difficult for me to break."

"You've invited men to the house again for dessert, haven't you?"

"Oh, honey, I was able to get Rita Winchester's son! I had to pull a lot of strings because he's usually booked solid this time of year."

"Booked solid? Do you even hear yourself?"

"If I cancel, Laura Kilroy will swoop right in!" said Mom. "Her daughter, Sophie, is finally home from Europe and she's been dying for the two of them to meet. The next time you come home, it'll be too late."

"Then I hope they're very happy together," I said, looking at the television as I marked down the item number on a swishy Lori Goldstein cardigan. I loved those layers. "Look, Mom, I've already told you why I don't date. Nothing's changed."

I had the urge to tell her the truth—that this sort of thing was part of the real reason I'd decided not to come home, and that the community dinner idea had only come later—but I couldn't bring myself to say it. I'd already told her that my not coming home was nothing personal, and this would only hurt her feelings. It wouldn't change anything, either. I'd been telling her for years to stop trying to fix me up with men, and she'd never listened. Like Amy, she had this twisted notion that I could be happy in *all* aspects of my life. I was happy in most of them, so why wasn't that enough? I had a beautiful house and a cool car; I helped my friends; I gave to charity. But when it came to emotions, and trust, and *love,* my money was a bull in a china shop. Even after the major humiliation that was Dean, nobody seemed to get that but me.

"But he's a plastic surgeon, Josie! He doesn't even *need* your money! Wasn't that the problem?"

"You'd be surprised what people suddenly decide they need after they get close to me."

"So, what? You're never going to date again? Is that it? You're just going to die a lonely old spinster? Look, honey, I know you trusted Dean and that he hurt you, but eventually you're going to have to let somebody else in."

"Says who?"

"Says the laws of attraction. When the right man comes along, you won't be *able* to fight it. You'll be like two wild animals. That's how it was with your father."

"Mom, ew." I squeezed my eyes shut, trying to dislodge the image. Pixie whimpered on the couch beside me. Even a dog knew how wrong that was. "You know, I never did say I was going to be *celibate*. I just can't have any expectations of a long-term commitment."

"Oh, Josephine."

"Can we please change the subject? Audrey and Randy are still coming for Thanksgiving, right?"

"Of course, they're coming," said Mom. "They wouldn't miss a free meal. Maybe I should send them up your way."

"Very funny."

"I suppose this means I'll have to do all the cooking again," she sighed.

"Feel free to hire a chef."

"It's too late for that," said Mom wistfully. "Maybe we should just book a cruise…"

"Or maybe you could see if Dad wants to cook."

"Your *father*?"

"Yes, my father. Learning to cook might give him something to do besides wandering up and down that beach looking for coins. Plus, it would be so adorable if you two cooked Thanksgiving dinner together. You could reignite that yucky animal attraction you speak of." Pixie flipped over onto her back, wiggling around until I rubbed her soft brown and white belly.

"Oh, that reminds me, I ordered a new patio set from Pottery Barn."

"How does that have anything to do with what I said?"

"You mentioned animals which reminded me of the zebra print pillows. You'll still be down for the Fourth of July, won't you? Or were you planning to grill up burgers and dogs for the townsfolk?"

"You're becoming very funny in your old age," I said, standing up and walking over to the back windows. A flock of turkeys strolled out of the woods, pecking around by the edge of the river. I've seen moose out there many times—actual moose, not the guy that owns the mini mart, which would be weird. Bears, too. My view of the river was one of the reasons I'd bought this house.

"Of course, I'll be down for the Fourth," I said, turning away from the window. "Is Dad around? Can you put him on?"

"Sweetheart," said Dad, coming on the line a moment later. "I still can't believe we won't be seeing you for Thanksgiving! Are you sure we can't come up and help?"

"No!" I said. If it was only my father who came, I wouldn't mind. But he would most certainly bring along everybody else, which would defeat half the purpose. I tried to soften my tone. "It's fine, Dad. It's only going to be a few people, if anybody even shows up at all."

"Well, okay," he said, sounding disappointed. "Let me know if anything changes. We don't keep much of a schedule around here. We can be up in a jiffy!"

"I will," I said. "Definitely." We chatted for a few more minutes before he put Mom back on the line.

"I have to go now, Mom. I need to stop by the local newspaper office to place the ad for my dinner."

"Can't you do that sort of thing online?" she asked.

"Not in Autumnboro. That's part of its charm."

"Don't tell me they have a little boy who runs around shouting 'Extra! Extra!'?"

"That would be so adorable!" I said, putting one hand on my

chest as I pictured him roaming up and down Main Street. The tourists would love it, and it might distract from the shoddy quality of the writing. Maybe I'd suggest it while I was over there. "I'll talk to you later, Mom. Love you!"

"You'll never meet a man in that town!" she shouted as I hung up the phone.

CHAPTER 7

⚜

The Autumnboro Times office was jammed into a small space between the senior center and The Soapy Gourd Laundromat. I pulled open the wooden door and stepped inside. The office was mostly quiet, except for the sound of a Zumba class coming through the wall on one side, and the chugging of washing machines on the other. A woman sat at a desk near the front of the office, staring intently at her computer. She had a pencil tucked behind her ear and several coffee cups on her desk, and seemed to be hard at work on a local news story. Seated across from her was a man with a similar setup, although, from the way he was clicking his mouse, I was pretty sure he was playing Minesweeper. They both ignored me. Further back in the office was a young man—he almost looked like a teenager from where I stood—lounging back in his chair, feet up on his desk. As soon as he noticed me, he shot up. A Rubik's cube tumbled out of his hands and onto the floor.

"Can I help you?" he asked.

"Yes, hi," I said. "I'd like to place an ad?"

"Sure thing," he said. "Come on back."

I walked past the other two employees—one of whom was, in

fact, playing Minesweeper—and sat down in the empty chair beside the ancient wooden desk. I picked up one of his business cards. Lee Moriarty, Advertising.

"Moriarty," I said, slipping the card into my purse. "Any relation to Moose?"

"Oh, yeah. He's my uncle. My mom told me if I didn't stay out of trouble and find myself a job by the end of the summer, I'd have to go work for Uncle Kyle at the mini mart. You'd better believe I grabbed this gig right quick." Lee fumbled around inside his desk, looking for a pen. Then he opened a drawer and pulled out what looked like a handwritten cheat sheet. He took a deep breath and started reading from the top. "Okay, first step. Name?"

"Josie Morgan."

He started to write it down, then paused and looked up at me. "Why do I know that name? Did we go to high school together?"

"Probably not. I'm slightly older than you. Maybe you know me from Pumpkin Everything? I'm the owner." I straightened up a bit in my chair, still absurdly proud every time I said it.

"Nah, that place is for old ladies," he said, shaking his head and looking back at his notepad. He finished writing down my name, spelling it with a *d* and two *e*'s, before I corrected him. "Okay, step two…"

"Isn't there a form I could just fill out?" I asked.

"There is *not*," he said loudly, glancing at the woman near the front of the office. She glanced back at him and rolled her eyes. "My high school newspaper was more advanced than this rag, but they don't want to take advice from a teenager. Anyway"—he cleared his throat—"what's the ad for?"

"It's an invitation to a free Thanksgiving dinner for anybody that needs a place to go. It's going to be held at the United Parish, here in Autumnboro, at one o'clock. On Thanksgiving Day, obviously. You can play around with the wording to make it sound good. You get the idea."

"Got it," said Lee. "When do you want it to run?"

"Soon," I said. "Can it possibly fit in this week's paper?"

Lee started laughing and tilting back in his chair. "Of *course*, it can fit. What else do you think we've got going on around here in Dullsville?" He motioned to the nearly empty office and, I assumed, the entire town beyond the door.

"If this town is so *dull*, what are you still doing here?" I teased. "Why didn't you go off to college?" Lee had a slight resemblance to his uncle—just around the eyes—and a familiar big, black tumbler on his desk. Someone in the Moriarty family must have been handing those things out for Christmas.

Lee snorted. "You sound like my uncle Kyle. I pretty much scraped through high school." He righted his chair and tapped his pen against the desk. "And that was with a bunch of teachers breathing down my neck, keeping me on track. Send me off to college, unsupervised?" He paused as he blew out a breath, flapping his lips. "You're just *asking* for trouble. It's not like I'm dumb or anything. I just need a tight leash. At least that's what my mom says."

"But your uncle thinks you should go?" That was surprising.

"He's got faith in me," said Lee, shrugging. "Don't ask me why. I guess it's because he doesn't have any kids of his own to bug. He's always on my case to *make something of myself*." He air-quoted the words.

"Nothing wrong with that," I said. "You know, you could always live at home and commute to college? That way your family could keep an eye on you. My friend Kit did that, and now he owns The Autumnboro Inn."

Lee looked at me like I had a giant, warty gourd growing out of my head. "You think I want to run an *inn*?"

"That's not what I meant. You could study whatever you wanted! Don't just write off college because your mom doesn't think you can handle it. What are you interested in?"

It was sort of funny that I was so staunchly promoting

college. I mean, *I'd* gone. I had a bachelor's degree in sociology, and worked for two years at a nonprofit down in Nashua, providing services to families in need. I loved it and I would have happily stayed on even after I'd won the lottery, but things became too difficult. My co-workers mostly stopped talking to me, and when they did, it was to make a snide remark about how much money I had and why I was still working at a place like that. Personally, I hadn't felt like I'd changed at all. I could still relate to everybody I worked with. I was still *me*, after all. But they hadn't felt the same. Plus, I had Mom in my ear, also asking why I wanted to work when I could just veg out with them. Eventually, I wrote the nonprofit a huge check, and I quit. Then Dean came along. Then Autumnboro. I don't exactly use my college degree these days, but I'm always glad that I have it.

"I don't really know what I'm interested in," said Lee, looking around the office. "Not *this*, I can tell you that much." The man sitting at the other desk gave him a dirty look.

"Well, there must be *something*," I said, resting my elbow on his desk and putting my chin in my hand. "If you had to pick a career, any career, what would it be?"

"Were you, like, a guidance counselor in another life?" asked Lee, looking at me quizzically.

"Sorry." I laughed. "I just like to talk. And I love meeting new people. *You're* new people."

"Lucky me," said Lee, picking up his Rubik's cube and spinning a few of the sides around. "Okay, well, I do kind of like the idea of teaching."

"Really? After what you just told me about high school?"

He nodded. "Those teachers that helped me were pretty cool. I'd be in an even worse job than this if I hadn't finished high school. Plus, you know, you get the summers off."

"I do know." I smiled. "My dad used to be a teacher, and he always joked that the best part of teaching was June, July, and

August. I think you should go for it. The world could certainly use some good teachers."

"Yeah, but how do you know I'd be good at it?" asked Lee. "There's a pretty high chance I'd stink. Then I'd *really* be letting Uncle Kyle down."

"Give yourself some credit!" I said. "And even if you did stink at it, I'm sure your uncle would be proud of you just for trying." I wasn't totally sure if that was true, but I had to assume Moose had a heart somewhere in his burly chest.

"Maybe," said Lee. "I just want to get out of this town someday, one way or another. Even if it's by moving to Summerboro. I hear it's lovely in the summer." He'd been working on the Rubik's cube the entire time he'd been talking, and with one last spin, solved it. He plunked it down in front of me.

"A friend of mine lives in Summerboro," I said, picking up the cube and inspecting it from all sides, impressed. "Believe it or not, I moved *to* Autumnboro *from* somewhere else. I love that it's small and quiet here, and that everyone knows everyone. Plus, I have wild animals in my backyard. How cool is that?"

"Yeah," he said, taking a swig from his black tumbler. "It's a real treat. Hang on while I write you up an invoice."

I sat quietly while he filled out a form with a carbon copy attached. All of a sudden, he stopped writing and looked up at me.

"Josie Morgan," he said slowly, his eyes widening. "Now I remember your name! You're the lottery winner!" The other two employees snapped their heads around to look at me.

"You got me." I shrugged. Now that he'd figured out who I was, he was probably going to add a few zeroes onto that invoice. That was okay. I'd been thinking about making an anonymous donation to the newspaper as soon as I'd walked in and seen the state of the carpets.

"Holy crap," he breathed, resuming the slouchy, laid-back position he was in when I'd arrived. He put his feet up on his desk and picked up the Rubik's cube, tossing it in the air. "That was a *ton* of money, lady. My uncle, he said you have more money than God and no clue what to do with it. No offense. And—hold on a second—" He sat up again, slamming the Rubik's cube back down on his desk. "You're telling me you won all that money and you moved *here*? Dude, you should be in Tahiti or Thailand or something!"

I snorted. "I'm staying far away from Thailand, trust me."

"Yeah? Why?"

"Long story." Amy had already forced part of the Dean saga out of me the other day. I wasn't about to lay it all on Moose's nephew in the middle of a newspaper office so it could end up on tomorrow's front page. "So, Lee, are we all set with the ad?"

"All set. I'll email you a proof. But, what *have* you done with all that dough? You must have done some crazy traveling before you ended up here. *Please* tell me you did some crazy traveling before you ended up here."

I opened my mouth and then closed it again.

"Oh, geez," said Lee.

"I've been to a few places," I said defensively, twisting my hair into a ponytail. "But now, I'm sort of…scared to travel. The flying, the hotels…it's not really my cup of tea. I *like* it here."

Lee just stared at me with pity in his eyes, which was new. I couldn't say that I liked it any more than jealousy.

"Dude," he said, "you're a gazillionaire. Even if your grandfather founded this lame town, you gotta get out of here at least for a vacation. Did you know that in Bora Bora you can stay in a hut that's like *on* the ocean? You could afford three of those things."

"Why would I possibly need three huts?" I asked, standing up. "Besides, Bora Bora has sharks, stingrays, and barracudas. Do you know what would happen to my money if I got eaten by a barracuda?"

"Your family would inherit it?"

"Exactly. Have you eaten lunch yet? Can I get you a sandwich? Or maybe a Maple Sugar Crush?"

"What the heck's a Maple Sugar Crush?"

"It's a frozen drink from The Shaky Maple."

"I've never set foot in that place. I like Dunkin. Did you know some old guy drove through the window last year? I had to switch to Starbucks for, like, a month."

"You should shop local. The Shaky Maple's great, and I've heard the Maple Sugar Crush is amazeballs."

"You're too old to be saying *amazeballs*, lady. But, sure. I could go for a coffee. Thanks."

"No problem," I said, heading for the door. "Back in a jiffy."

As I stepped outside, I tried for a moment to see the town from Lee's perspective. Sure, it was small, and there wasn't too much going on in the way of news. But he didn't have a clue what it was like to be me. Having this sort of money was unfathomable, as it was to most people. Sure, it might seem surprising, and maybe a bit pitiful, that I'd never done much traveling. But I had my reasons. I could get by without travel or dating. Believe me, it was a small price to pay for being a gazillionaire.

CHAPTER 8

When I walked into Pumpkin Everything on Friday morning, Tom had a newspaper in his hand, and a worried look on his face.

"There you are," he said, as soon as I'd opened the door. "Thank goodness."

"What's wrong?" I asked, letting Pixie off her leash, and hurrying over to where he was leaning against the counter. I cringed as a thought occurred to me. "The life-sized Santa didn't get delivered early, did it?"

"The life-sized *what*?"

"Never mind. What's wrong?"

He shook the newspaper. "I know you said you wanted to host a community dinner, and I know I said it was a good idea, but Josie…do you think this is wise? You're going to get quite a turnout."

Quite a turnout? I'd almost forgotten that my ad was supposed to run today in *The Autumnboro Times*. I grabbed the newspaper out of his hands and scanned the page until I found it.

ALONE FOR THE HOLIDAYS? DON'T BE!
JOIN US FOR A FREE THANKSGIVING DINNER AT
THE UNITED PARISH OF AUTUMNBORO
ALL ARE WELCOME! NOBODY TURNED AWAY!
DATE: NOVEMBER 25
TIME: ONE O'CLOCK

"OKAY," I said, not quite understanding what the problem was. "That looks fine to me. Maybe a little dull. I thought I told Lee to play around with the wording?" I sighed and shook my head.

"Josie, darling, this isn't *The Autumnboro Times*," said Tom. "It's the *Portsmouth Herald*. I picked up a copy this morning because Barbara said there was a coupon inside to Applebee's."

"*What?*"

The *Portsmouth Herald* circulated way, way, *way* south of here. Like, down by Kittery. *Oh, Lee. What did you do?* I dropped the newspaper on the counter and grabbed the business card I'd pinned to the bulletin board. I punched in the number.

"Lee?" I practically shouted, as soon as he'd said hello. "This is Josie Morgan. From the other day?"

"Oh, hey, Josie! I was just about to call and thank you. That Maple Sugar Crush was amazeballs, just like you said. You are officially allowed to use that word. I went and got another one yesterday. Haven't slept in days, but it's totally worth it. What's up?"

"What's *up*? How about printing my ad in the *Portsmouth Herald?*" I jabbed at the newspaper, as if he could see.

"What are you talking about?"

"I'm talking about the ad for my small, local dinner being advertised in *another part of the state*! How did that even happen?" There were a few seconds of silence on the other end of the line.

"Oh, crap," he finally said.

"What?"

"Well, the *Portsmouth Herald* is one of our sister companies. I… I must have emailed it over to them by accident. The advertising lady over there, her name is Jessica, which is similar to *Jennifer*, who's the lady that does the layout over here in my office, and you know how autofill can be…"

"Oh, Lee."

"Look, I've been a little jittery lately! It's your fault! You got me hooked on those coffees!"

"You cannot possibly be blaming this on me!"

"What's the big deal, anyway?" asked Lee. "You're loaded! Why not rent out a big hall or a tent or something? It'll be awesome. I'd go. Need a DJ?" I held the phone away from my ear as he started beat-boxing and drumming on his desk. I waited until someone in the office yelled at him to shut up. Probably Jennifer.

"The big deal is that this was supposed to be a small, quiet dinner, for people who live in *Autumnboro*. If I wanted to deal with a mob of people hounding me for money, I'd have just gone home to see my family."

"But how are they even going to know you have a lot of money?"

"Because, Lee, everybody in this town knows about my money. And all anybody from out of town has to do is to start chatting with the locals over their turkey dinner." I pinched the bridge of my nose and looked over at Tom, who had been pretending to organize the old-fashioned stick candy. He looked back at me, his fluffy white eyebrows furrowed. My name and hometown had both been made public after I'd won the lottery, so it wasn't like I'd been living some secretive, anonymous life-style or anything. But after moving up here to Autumnboro, my life had managed to remain pretty quiet. It was mostly just family that came around now, looking for cash. This dinner could potentially change all that.

"Gee Josie, I'm sorry," said Lee. "I didn't do it on purpose. Do you want to call off the whole thing?"

I sighed. Did I want to call off the whole thing? Not really. Even with the risk it posed, that didn't change the facts I'd read in that newspaper article. People were alone and sad on Thanksgiving, and I wanted to help them. Now there were people from all around the state who'd seen my ad. Their spirits may have already been lifted at the news that they wouldn't have to be alone this year.

"No," I said. "I don't want to cancel it. It is what it is."

"Are you sure? You're not going to tell my boss, are you?"

"I'm not going to tell your boss," I said, rolling my eyes and running my hand through my hair. I had to remind myself that Lee was just a kid who'd only chosen a job at the newspaper to avoid working at his uncle's mini mart, and who could blame him for that? This would be a learning experience. "Hey, have you given any more thought to what we talked about? About college?"

"A little," he said, sounding relieved that I'd changed the subject. "I looked at a few schools online last night."

"That's great!"

"Sure, it is, until you look at how much they actually *cost.* How am I supposed to pay for that?"

I smiled at the fact that he'd completely forgotten who he was talking to.

"There are ways," I said. "Trust me. Hey, I have to go. I have a huge dinner to plan, remember? I'll see you around, Lee."

"Yeah, okay. See ya, lady."

I hung up the phone, looked at Tom, and put my face in my hands.

"Soup's on, eh?" said Tom.

I nodded without looking up.

* * *

So, this had gotten a little out of hand. Five turkeys weren't going to cut it anymore. I knew I should have listened to my gut and ordered fifteen. The church basement wasn't going to be big enough, either. I googled the *Portsmouth Herald* and saw that it had a circulation of almost ten thousand. Ten thousand! The only place I could think to hold this thing, on short notice, would be out in the middle of the town common. It was still close enough to the church that people would be able to find it, and I'd be able to fit as many tables and chairs as I could rent. I'd also probably have to get a permit from Town Hall in order to hold an event there. An *event.* How had my small good deed turned into an *event?* I was also going to have to rent buffet tables, and those warming trays you put all the food in. Plus, outdoor heaters and portable toilets. I couldn't forget the toilets.

I actually wouldn't mind doing any of this, if it weren't for the threat of the few lousy people who might try to take advantage of me. But I was determined not to let the bad apples ruin this for all the good guys. Thanksgiving was about being thankful for what you had, and I couldn't think of a better way to show my gratitude for what I was given—even if it did sometimes have its downsides—than by sharing it with those less fortunate. The idea of this dinner had given me something to look forward to, rather than the usual stress and anxiety of an upcoming Thanksgiving dinner with my family. It would all work out.

"I'm heading out for a few minutes," I said to Tom. I needed to take a walk to clear my head, and maybe get some caffeine. I took Pixie across the street to The Shaky Maple. The large, colorful chalkboard behind the counter had been updated with its November theme. Someone with a lot of talent had drawn a turkey holding a coffee cup in the center of the board, with pilgrim hats and cornucopias in each corner. The list of specialty lattes had been updated to include pecan pie, gingerbread, and peppermint mocha.

"Maple Sugar Crush, please," I said to the barista. So, that was a definite yes to the caffeine, especially after Lee had gone and planted the idea in my head. As long as I wasn't anywhere near QVC, it should be okay. "Actually, make it two."

I should probably bring one over to Riley and tell him I wasn't going to be able to use the church basement after all. I felt a prickle of anticipation at the thought of seeing him again, even though the feeling was most definitely not mutual.

By the time I arrived at the funeral home, my hands were like ice cubes from carrying two frozen coffees. Maggie wasn't at her desk, which was good, since I hadn't brought her anything to drink, but also bad, since she was my buffer any time conversation with Riley became awkward. Not that it mattered. I'd just hand him the coffee, tell him the news—maybe catch a whiff of his aftershave—and be on my way. There was no need to stick around, talking his ear off, like I had all summer.

I placed the cups down on Maggie's desk, rubbed my frozen hands together, and looked around. As many times as I'd been inside the funeral home, it still gave me the creeps. I mean, it's *lovely*, in its own way. Lots of floral artwork, dimly lit lamps, and vases full of faux flowers. There's a tissue box on every end table, and the restroom is always immaculate. The couches are a bit stiff, but it's not like people come in here to hang out and watch TV. Overall, it's nice. It's just really, really…quiet.

"Riley?" I called out. Pixie barked.

I knew where his office was, and could have easily walked straight to it, but dogs aren't officially allowed in here. Besides, I have this fear of accidentally bumping into a corpse. Like, a corpse laid out in a casket? Yes. Or, also, a reanimated corpse roaming the hallways looking for its family. My fear has no parameters. Riley once told me that they do all the dead body stuff in a totally different part of the building (a building which is not very big to begin with, so not comforting *at all*), but I still wasn't crazy about the idea of just strolling around willy-nilly, like I was at the mall.

"Riley?" I called out again, louder, my voice echoing off the walls. Maybe he wasn't even here. What if *nobody* was here and the door locked behind me and I had to stay here all night? I picked up a pamphlet from the corner of Maggie's desk, trying to distract myself. On the cover was a smiling elderly woman reading through her own funeral documents, which totally didn't help.

"You know, you could have just come straight down to my office," said Riley, making me jump as he walked into the room. Before he'd grown some facial hair, he used to look a bit like one of those roaming corpses I'd been so nervous about. He never seemed to get enough sun. But now, that scruffy beard was doing wonders for him. The butterflies in my stomach swirled right up into one of those big, scary insect tornados. The kind that keep me from ever moving to the Midwest.

"Hey," I said, quickly shoving the pamphlet back into its holder. It got stuck halfway and made a big crease down the middle of the elderly woman's face. "Sorry about that."

"It's fine. You can keep that, if you want. Hey, Pixie." He reached down and petted her on the head as she stretched up his black pant leg, leaving a trail of white dog hair behind.

"No, thanks," I said, gently tugging Pixie's leash so she'd come back to me. "Here. I brought you a coffee." I handed it to him, trying to remain as cold and emotionless as possible. But the way his face lit up at the sight of that coffee, I totally melted inside.

"Thanks," he said, taking a long sip, his eyes still on me. It was awfully hot in here, for a funeral home. "What's the occasion?"

"No occasion," I said, perching on the edge of Maggie's desk. "Well, except for the fact that I accidentally invited half the world to my Thanksgiving dinner. That's what I came by to tell you. The church basement isn't going to work anymore. But thank you for trying."

He raised his eyebrows. "How the heck did you do that?"

"It's a long story," I said, sliding back off the desk. I didn't know why I'd gone and sat up there, anyway. I seemed to be quickly falling back into my old routine of making small talk with someone who clearly wasn't interested. "And you probably need to get back to work. I'll see you later, Riley."

Before he could reply, Pixie and I were out the door.

CHAPTER 9

J'd almost made it to the sidewalk, when I heard Riley's voice behind me.

"Wait."

I stopped and turned cautiously around. "Yes?"

He'd stopped only a few feet away, and was holding up his coffee cup. "Does this mean we're doing this again?"

"Doing what again?"

"You know…you coming by with a Maple Sugar Crush, us going out for walks. It was sort of like…our thing."

Pixie's ears perked up at the word *walk,* mine at the words *our thing.* Had that really been our thing? It sure sounded nice, even if I wouldn't have described it that way. But if Riley thought it was our thing, then hey…sign me up.

"Um, yeah," I said. "Sure. If you want to. I didn't even think you'd noticed when I stopped coming."

"Of course, I noticed."

"I'm sure you missed the free coffees," I pressed on, pausing to glare at a Budget rental truck speeding around the common. "But I'm sure you didn't miss me blabbing away in your ear while you were trying to concentrate on your game."

"I liked the company."

"Oh," I said, completely thrown by this statement. "You, um, you never seemed very chatty. So, I…I didn't know." Pixie looked up at me and barked, as if to ask why we hadn't yet moved along to somewhere warm. I crouched down to pet her, avoiding eye contact with Riley.

"I'm not very chatty with anyone," he said, rubbing the back of his neck and gazing off across the common. Then he looked down at me, his brows knit together. "Wait. Is that why you stopped coming?"

The smart thing to do would be to say yes. What the smart thing *wouldn't* be would be telling him the truth. Unfortunately, the truth had been bubbling up inside of me for months, and apparently there was no stopping it now.

"Sort of," I said, standing up. "Look, I can take a hint, Riley. I *saw* how you looked when you were actually having a good time with someone. And you never once looked that way when you were hanging out, walking around town, with me. So…that's why I stopped coming."

"Who'd you see me having such a great time with?"

"Nobody. Forget it."

"It couldn't have been Kit or Amy. Those two make me nauseous these days."

"It wasn't them." I laughed. I'd had the same thought, but been too polite to say it. "I saw you with, um, Catrina. Catrina Corman. One time." I cringed as the words came out of my mouth, but it was too late now. There they were. Riley gave me an odd look. "What?" I asked.

"When did you see me with *her*?"

"Oh, I don't remember," I said breezily, trying to play it down. "It was just one day over the summer. I was passing by and I saw you two on the, um"—I coughed—"the tire swings."

"Oh, *that*," he said, almost laughing as he shoved his free hand into his pants pocket and took a step back. "I was trying to get

Darlene Murphy a better deal on a headstone, so I bought Catrina a coffee and told her to meet me on the common. She's a goofball. I figured acting like one too might butter her up a little."

"Did it work?"

"I wasn't voted Autumnboro's best funeral planner for nothing."

"Aren't you the *only* funeral planner in Autumnboro?"

"You're funny."

I smiled. "Well then, Riley, you're a great salesman, and an even better actor." My spirits lifted at the fact that he hadn't actually been enjoying himself with Catrina, and that maybe my only competition was that five-inch rectangle in his pocket (totally not a euphemism). Of course, competition was only a thing if you were trying to *win* at something, which I wasn't. The only reason I'd come here was to tell Riley about the dinner—which I'd already done—so I should really get going. "I'll see you around. Come on, Pix." I turned to leave.

"I have to run some paperwork over to Town Hall," Riley called after me. "Want to come?"

I stopped in my tracks. Of *course,* I wanted to come. And, I mean, if he was going over there anyway, what was the harm? It wasn't like it was a date or something. It was just a walk to a government building. I'd walked to Town Hall with ninety-year-old Ed Woodbury when he'd needed a copy of his wife's death certificate, and we hadn't fallen in love with each other.

"Okay" I said. "Sure. I'll come."

As we walked, I gave him the full story of how Lee had managed to so royally mess up my ad. From there, I told him about how shocked Lee had been when he learned I'd never done much traveling.

"I mean, just because someone has a lot of money, why does that mean they have to travel? I spent a lot of money on my house. I'm not just going to *leave* it to get all dusty and stuffy while I go traveling around the globe."

"You could hire a maid?"

"That's not the point."

"I thought it was?"

"The point is that I have plenty to do right here in Autumn-boro. I have the store, and the inn, and volunteering at the senior center. And one of these days Moose is going to offer me a job."

"And I thought *I* was the introvert," said Riley.

"What's that supposed to mean?"

"I mean, I'm the one who likes to stay home. You're the extro-vert, Josie. You would *love* traveling and meeting new people."

I just shrugged.

"You told me once," he said, glancing over at me, "that you don't travel because you have a fear of flying, and a fear of boats, and what was it? Travel diarrhea?"

I nodded solemnly. That was nothing to joke about.

"So, which is it? Are you too busy to travel, or do you have a bunch of phobias?"

"Can't it be both?"

"Maybe. But it sounds more like a bunch of mixed-up excuses. What's your deal?"

What's your deal? Just the words a girl wants to hear from her crush.

"What do you mean?"

"I mean, if you actually do have all those phobias, how'd you get them? They don't just come out of nowhere."

"Well, maybe they're not exactly, one hundred percent *phobias*," I said, bobbing my head back and forth. "Okay? Maybe I just tell people that because it's easier than explaining the truth."

"Which is?"

We were coming up on Pumpkin Everything, and I came to a stop in front of the store. A *Back in 10 Minutes* sign had been taped to the door. I'd never told this to anybody before. Maybe because nobody had ever asked, maybe because I knew how nuts I would sound. But, for some reason—just as the truth about

Catrina Corman had bubbled up—I suddenly wanted Riley to know.

"Come on inside for a minute." I unlocked the door and Riley followed me in. It was quiet inside the store, the scent of all the fall spices both warm and welcoming.

"I can't remember the last time I was in here," said Riley, picking up a little log cabin incense burner from the shelf by the door.

April third, I thought, walking over and leaning against the counter. "So, you want to know the truth?"

He put the log cabin down and nodded. "Lay it on me."

"Okay, this is going to sound nuts," I said, "but hear me out. After I won the lottery, it was like this weird sort of survival instinct kicked in. Like, I realized that if I were to die, all of my money would go to my parents and my sister. Which seems like a good thing on the surface, right? I'm sure they'd be happy about it, aside from the whole me being dead part."

"So, you don't want your family to inherit your money?"

"It sounds *terrible* when you say it out loud, doesn't it? But I just…I have this fear that they wouldn't be able to handle it. Like, with me, it's fine. I haven't blown it all yet. I try my best to use it for good deeds. I've managed to remain grounded and sane." Riley made a face that made me laugh. "*Relatively* grounded and sane, okay?"

"Okay."

"But anyone else?" I continued. "This money could totally ruin their lives. It could turn them into greedy, superficial spend-thrifts, just like my aunt and uncle and—" I stopped myself before saying his name. "Anyway, even if they managed to remain nice, normal people, all the gold-digging relatives would turn their attention on my parents, which isn't how they deserve to spend their retirement. And what about my sister and my brother-in-law? They have young kids, and they've finally opened their dream business. Do you think they want to deal with distant relatives from Oklahoma asking for money for Lasik eye surgery?

"Probably not?"

"No, they don't. So, what it comes down to is that I've been avoiding anything that might make me die. Travel. Thrill rides. I've completely cut out romaine lettuce."

If we're being completely honest, my fears didn't start *right* after I'd won the lottery. It was more like right after Dean had landed in Bangkok and I'd realized how easily money could bring out the worst in people.

"Word around town is that you still use Ludicrous Mode," said Riley. "Isn't that dangerous?"

"You leave my car out of this," I said, pointing one finger at him. Okay, sure, maybe going zero to sixty in under three seconds was slightly dangerous. But it was my one exception. I wasn't a *total* bore.

"Okay." He laughed, holding up his hands. "Sorry. Why don't you just bequeath everything to Pixie? That would solve your problems."

Now it was my turn to laugh. "You've just given me a great idea for April Fool's Day."

"Seriously, though," he said, his face turning thoughtful. "You should have more faith in your family, Josie. They raised *you*, after all. I'm sure they'd figure it all out, just like you did."

"I don't know that for sure," I said, shaking my head. "Money warps people, Riley. Trust me. I should know."

"And how *do* you know?" he asked, his dark, intense eyes boring into me. "What happened to you, Moneybags?"

"Just…you know…greedy relatives." I shrugged. "Don't you have to get to Town Hall? I think Pixie and I will just stay here." Pixie had already made herself comfortable on a chair by the fireplace and wouldn't be moving again until dinnertime.

"Right," he said, his expression lightening up a bit. "Town Hall. I'd better get going. Thanks again for the coffee."

"Any time," I said. "See ya, Riley."

The door closed behind him, and I watched him walk past the window, imagining—for a moment—what would happen if I chased after him. If I stopped him, spun him around, kissed him right out there on the sidewalk. Would he push me away? Would he pull me closer? My whole body tensed at the possibilities. He was suddenly being so friendly, but at the same time, he was still so hard to read. *Just stop it, Josie.* I blew out a breath and turned away from the window.

It didn't matter. Riley and I could be friends, and that was it. That had been my intention at the beginning of the summer, and it wasn't his fault that I now had the world's biggest, stupidest crush on him. I just had to keep my feelings under control. Because if I ever let my guard down again—if I ever let myself think that maybe Riley and I could be a *thing*, and that there was no way he'd ever hurt me—then, BOOM! Just like that, he'd be gone again.

I knew it.

CHAPTER 10

*E*very year, before Grayson's Turkey Farm closed down their ice cream stand for the winter, they gave away everything that was left for free. The only condition was that you had to order a small-sized cup, and you had to wait in line all over again if you wanted seconds. Amy, Kit, and Tom were all leaving for Pennsylvania tomorrow, but luckily, they were still around for today's big event. I was meeting the three of them, plus Riley, in half an hour at the farm.

Grayson's Turkey Farm was actually more of a family fun center than a farm. Located on the outskirts of Autumnboro, it had batting cages, bumper boats, a driving range, and a beautifully designed miniature golf course, which was very popular during the summer months. In the fall, they drew a good crowd with their corn maze, pumpkin patch, and hay rides. Everything was closed now, except for the restaurant and the farm store—which were both open year-round—and the ice cream stand. The line for free ice cream extended halfway into the parking lot, even though it was only forty degrees outside. The five of us huddled in a tight pack at the back of the line. Pixie was wearing her warmest coat—a black and red buffalo check number—and was excited enough about the words *ice cream* that she didn't seem too bothered by the cold.

"We used to have all our sports banquets here when we were kids," said Riley. Since it was Saturday, he'd traded in his formal work attire for a black North Face jacket over a hooded sweatshirt, and jeans. Every time we bumped elbows—which seemed to be happening a lot more than it should have—I forced myself to think unsexy thoughts. Cabbage stew. Armpit hair. Diapers. It didn't seem to be helping.

"You played sports?" I asked, taking a tiny step closer to Tom. Even in his casual clothing, the only sports I could picture Riley playing were on an Xbox. But even that seemed sort of adorable. So *him*.

"Soccer," he said. "Third grade."

"Ah." Now I was picturing a nine-year-old Riley tromping around a soccer field, which was also adorable. Heaven help me.

"People sure love free stuff," said Kit, furrowing his brow at the line of people ahead of us. I could see a few teenaged girls in the windows, taking orders as quickly as they could.

"You think there'll be anything left by the time we get up there?" asked Amy.

"I haven't eaten all day," said Tom. "If I don't get some Muddy Moose soon, I might pass out."

"Why didn't you *eat*?" asked Amy. "I stocked your fridge two days ago! Please don't tell me it's gone already."

"You stocked it with all that hippy dippy organic stuff. I wanted a bologna sandwich."

"You know where you can get a bologna sandwich?" asked Amy. "The dining room at Winter's Eve Assisted Living."

"Very funny."

"Everybody relax," I said. "If they run out of ice cream—take it easy, Pix—we'll go over to Sweet Something in Summerboro. My treat. I'm sure they'd love the business."

If you think Autumnboro becomes depressing after

Halloween, you should see poor Summerboro. I don't know what the founding fathers were thinking when they named that town, but there's a very small window for drinking piña coladas by a lake when you're located in northern New Hampshire.

"Why don't we just go to Sweet Something right now?" asked Tom. "Instead of standing around here freezing to death?"

"Because this is an Autumnboro tradition!" said Amy. Ever since she'd apologized to the town for ripping them apart in her horror novels, Amy's been pretty serious about preserving local traditions. "Look, the line's moving." We shuffled forward a few steps and then stopped again.

To be honest, as much as I enjoyed the social aspect of free ice cream day, I felt sort of weird taking anything from the Grayson's for free. That family worked their butts off on this farm, and I could certainly afford to help them out. I opened my wallet to check how much cash I had on me, then I craned my neck to see if they had any tip jars up there. Riley's eyes were on me as I pulled out five twenties.

"What?"

"You don't have to do that," he said, nodding toward the cash. "Everyone else is taking as much as they can get, without a second thought."

"Well I'm not *like* everybody else," I said. "I feel weird taking it for free. Especially if there are other people who need it more than me."

"Nobody *needs* free ice cream."

"You know what I mean," I said. "The funny thing is that if anyone sees me slipping these twenties into the tip jar, they'll probably talk about how I think I'm better than everybody else." By *anyone*, I meant Moose. I'd spotted him in the other line, a few people up.

Eventually, we made it up to the order window where Tom got his Muddy Moose, I got my cup of coffee Oreo, and Pixie got a "pup cup" of vanilla soft serve. Just as I was about to drop the twenties into the tip jar, Riley stepped up beside me, leaning his elbow on the counter and blocking me from view. I dropped the money in, as good as anonymous.

"Slick," I said. "Thanks."

"Any time."

The five of us took our ice cream to an empty picnic table and sat down. Pixie jumped into my lap as soon as I'd placed her cup on the table, and started licking away.

"You know what?" said Tom, after we'd all finished our second servings and were well on our way to freezing to death. "I just realized I forgot to take my medication."

"Oh, no!" said Amy. "What should we do?"

"We'd better get him home," said Kit. "Straight away."

"Right," said Amy. "We'd better go. All of us, except for you, Josie. You, too, Riley. There's no reason for you two to leave, just because Grandpa goofed up." Tom shot her a look that I'm pretty sure wasn't a part of their terribly scripted performance. Was she for real? My cheeks, despite the cold, started to burn.

"That's okay," I said, giving her a stern look. "It's freezing out, and I have laundry to do. And Pixie wants to go home."

"Or we could stay," said Riley. I turned to look at him, my stomach flipping over as his dark brown eyes, framed by the hood of his sweatshirt, latched onto mine. "We could play some Pokémon Go."

We. Riley and me, together. Doing a thing. Why did it always have to sound so nice?

"I can take Pixie for you," said Tom. "*Sharyn's Closet* is on in half an hour. We'll curl up in front of the TV and take a nap." At the word *nap,* Pixie jumped off my lap and ran to Tom, licking his hand. Traitor.

"Okay," I said, giving Amy a subtle dirty look. "Fine. We'll stay."

While a big part of me wanted to wring her neck for this scheme she'd concocted, another part—the part that contained all the hormones I'd been doing a fairly good job of keeping under control until Riley crept back into my life—wanted to give her a hug, and a high-five. And maybe a couple million bucks.

* * *

"Where to?" I asked Riley, after everyone had left. We were standing awkwardly in the parking lot as most of the other cars continued to pull out. He looked at the map on his phone.

"It looks like there are a bunch over by the mini golf. We could start there."

"Okay."

The rest of the farm was totally deserted. I was pretty sure we weren't supposed to be traipsing around looking for cartoon characters, but I followed after him anyway. Roy Grayson would probably let me do anything I wanted on his farm, as long as I kept ordering pies every year. Sometimes it struck me just how much power I actually had, if I ever wanted to use it. Or abuse it. I liked to think I was doing a pretty good job of staying grounded. Gandalf could have totally entrusted me with the ring.

I sat down on the low stone wall that surrounded the miniature golf course, while Riley tapped away at his phone. The stone was freezing cold and went right through my jeans. I looked up at the surrounding mountains. Loon was the closest, and if I turned around to the north, I could see the back of Mt. Liberty. To the west was Moosilauke—the tenth highest of New Hampshire's 4,000-footers. Last fall, Amy had been shocked when she found out I didn't know the names of all the surrounding mountains, so she'd given me a crash course.

I zipped my coat all the way up to my chin and buried my face inside. It would have been much warmer if the sun were out, but it was hiding behind the building clouds and there was the definite feeling of snow in the air. I looked up, hoping to see those first few flakes wafting down. Nothing yet.

"Find anything good?" I asked, after several more minutes of silence. All the warm feelings I'd been having about Riley were starting to freeze over, along with my butt. Sometimes I wanted to throw that phone of his straight into the Pemi.

"Not really," he said, surprising me by shoving his phone into his pocket and sitting down on the wall beside me. "To be honest, I didn't actually see too many on the map. I, um, I just wanted to get you alone for a few minutes."

"Oh?"

My mouth was suddenly dry, as my heart started hammering away in my chest. So, maybe all those warm feelings I'd been having had been warranted after all. Warranted, but still highly unhelpful. What was I even doing? Why hadn't I just gone home with Pixie to do laundry? Nothing that happened from here on out was going to end well. I mean, it might *feel* great, but later? Terrible.

"Josie, I just wanted to ask you—"

"Do you want to play?" I interrupted, motioning to the minia-ture golf course.

"Huh?"

"Mini golf. Do you want to play?"

Please say yes. I needed to do something to keep Riley from making a move that I would have to try, and most definitely fail, to reject.

"I'm pretty sure mini golf is closed for the season," he said.

"Ah, but you're not the only one with connections," I said. I took out my phone and dialed the main number for the turkey farm. Luckily, it was Roy who answered, and a few minutes later we watched as he came out the back of the ice cream stand and walked to the building attached to the mini golf course. After a moment, he came out a side door carrying clubs and balls. Blue and pink.

"I'm sorry I can't turn on the waterfall or the windmill or anything," he said, handing us the clubs. "But you two are still welcome to play. If anyone asks why you're allowed out here and they aren't, I'll just tell them who you are. Britney Spears gets to skip the lines at Disney, right?"

"We'll just try to be inconspicuous," I said, wincing at the thought of Roy telling everybody that I'd bought my way onto his mini golf course. People wouldn't even consider the fact that I'd done it by buying charity pies. They never do.

I kept Riley distracted for the first three holes, talking about anything and everything that came to mind. But it was on the way to hole four that Riley stopped in the middle of the concrete path and turned to me.

"Josie, I really need to ask you something."

I took a deep breath as I looked up at him, framed against the backdrop of a bleak November sky. Riley had never been the type to light up a room, but he certainly had the power to switch something on inside of *me*. How was I supposed to fight this? Maybe Amy, and my mother, had been right; maybe I *should* give Riley a chance. Maybe there were some animal attractions that you just couldn't resist, no matter what. And, if there was anybody that I could trust not to be after my money, at least not right off the bat, it was him.

"Yes?" I took a step closer. He seemed nervous. What was he going to say? That he'd had a crush on me all summer? That he couldn't live another minute without me?

Thank you, Amy, for making this happen.

"So, there's this, um, Pokémon Go challenge starting in Japan next year."

Wait…what? I took a step back. "Okay…"

"People are coming from all over the world to play, Josie. It starts in Tokyo, and then you hop flights all over the world, country to country, chasing down Pokémon! The prizes this year are insane!" His eyes lit up as he spoke, just as I felt mine rapidly starting to dim.

"That sounds…amazing?" I said.

Pokémon? Seriously? Why had he made such a big deal out of telling me this? Maybe he was about to ask me to go with him. Sure, we'd be staring at our phones the entire time, and there was no way I was ever getting on an airplane, but the *idea* of it was romantic. It was the thought that would count.

"It is amazing, Josie," he said, taking a step closer to me and putting his hands on my shoulders, which was all sorts of confusing. He gently led me over to the stone wall. We sat down again, and he angled his body toward me, our legs touching. "It's *really* amazing, and it's a once-in-a-lifetime sort of thing. It's the sort of thing that you want to experience when you're young."

"Uh huh," I said, gazing into his eyes.

"The only problem is…"

"Yes?"

"I can't afford to go."

A knot formed in my stomach. "Oh?"

"I could save the money up, if I had more time. It's just that this thing starts in January."

I felt lightheaded and sick as understanding sank in.

"You want…money," I said, practically in a whisper. *Duh.*

"Just a loan," he added quickly. "I'll pay you back, of course. Don't worry."

I glared at him, a lump forming in my throat. My whole body suddenly chilled. I'd really done a bang-up job convincing myself that he wasn't about to ask for money. I'd known better, and yet I'd still gone and let myself hope—for just a moment—that Riley was different. I'd actually thought that maybe I should give him a chance. Stupid, stupid, *stupid*.

"You think I care about you *paying it back?*" I asked, incredulous. I slid off the wall and took a few steps away.

He raised his eyebrows. "You mean, you'd just give it to me? Like a gift?"

I opened my mouth and then snapped it shut again. Anger at my own stupidity was quickly turning into anger at Riley.

"No! Not like a gift!" I spat back. "Are you out of your mind? All that talk about missing how I used to bring you coffee, and wanting to go on walks with me again. Pretending like we'd had a *thing*! You were just buttering me up! You were buttering me up like Catrina Corman!" I couldn't believe this. I was going to *kill* Amy.

"That's not true!" he protested. "I mean, yeah, sure, I was trying to be friendlier so it wouldn't be so out of the blue when I asked you. But that doesn't mean—"

"Oh, please," I cut in. "You don't have to pretend that this is anything more than it is, Riley Parker. It's not like I'm not used to it. Men have been after my money for years now. You're not special."

I took off in the direction of the parking lot, when I realized I was still carrying my golf club and ball. I turned around, walked back to Riley, and shoved both of them into his chest.

"Make sure these get back to Roy," I said. I turned and started to head off again, before stopping one more time and calling over my shoulder, "And tell him I said thank you. That was very kind of him."

Then I was off, like a whirlwind, for real.

CHAPTER 11

I stopped my car in front of the mailbox and pulled out a pile of envelopes addressed to Kit Parker and The Autumnboro Inn. Tossing them onto the passenger seat, I continued up the driveway. I'd been thrilled when Kit and Amy asked if I would stop by the inn to bring in the mail and water the plants while they were away. It was the most involvement I'd had with the inn so far, and I'd almost brought over some Joan Rivers Christmas ornaments for the tree, but decided against it. I was a *silent* partner, and I needed to accept that. When it came down to it, Kit—much like his conniving younger brother—had only been interested in my money. Surprise, surprise.

The sky was much brighter today than it had been over the weekend—the threat of snow gone, at least for now—though my mood was anything but sunny. I'd avoided running into Riley yesterday (didn't leave the house), but today was Monday and I'd needed to open the store. I figured that as long as I stayed away from the funeral home and The Shaky Maple, everything would be okay. I couldn't imagine Riley barging into Pumpkin Everything to try to continue our discussion. I thought I'd made it pretty clear that I wasn't giving him a nickel for his trip.

The funny thing is, if he'd just stayed his normal, moody self, and asked me for the money out of the blue, I would have given it to him in a heartbeat. But he'd been toying with my emotions. Playing me. *Buttering me up* like a naïve piece of toast. Sure, he probably didn't know that I had a major crush on him—and if he did, please shoot me now—but did that even matter? That wasn't the way you treated people. The fact that he'd done it before to Catrina Corman, to get a better deal on a headstone, was a red flag I totally should've seen. Live and learn…again.

I let Pixie out of the car and headed for the front porch, fishing the key out of my purse as I walked.

"Pixie! Stop!" I cried, looking up in time to see her lift her leg and urinate on the antique garden statue Kit and Amy had brought back from Vermont. I used to think that only boy dogs did that sort of thing, but nope. "Aw, man."

I left the mail on the reception desk inside, then went back out to hose off the statue and water the plants. I was just getting ready to lock up, when my cell phone rang.

"Meg!" I said, answering the call. I was always happy to hear from my sister. "What's up?"

"Why didn't you tell us?"

"Tell you what?" I asked, turning the bolt on the front door and heading back to my car.

"About the big dinner! Mom said you were hosting some tiny thing for homeless people and senior citizens. Then I saw the ad in the newspaper all the way over here! Why didn't you tell us it was such a big event?"

"Woah, woah, woah. How did *you* see the ad?" The *Portsmouth Herald* circulated down by the Maine border, but Meg was in Kennebunkport, which was way up the coast.

"A customer left a copy at the café this morning and I happened to flip it open. When I saw the name 'Autumnboro' I knew it had to be you!"

I groaned as I let Pixie into the car. "That was a mistake, Meg.

That ad was supposed to run in the *local* newspaper. Now it's apparently spreading all over two states."

"Wow, that stinks," said Meg, an espresso machine grinding away loudly in the background. "Can I do anything to help? I could come down for a few days, leave Dave in charge of the café and the kids…"

"That's sweet, but not necessary. I don't want you dropping everything for me." If Meg came, then my dad would surely follow, along with the rest of them.

"Are you sure?"

"Totally."

"You could call off the whole thing, you know? Come down to the Cape, like normal? The girls are pretty bummed that you won't be there."

"I can't," I said. "There was a reason I'd planned this dinner in the first place, Meg, and that hasn't changed. If anybody has the means to handle this sort of thing, it's me, right?"

"Well, yeah," she said, her voice filled with uncertainty. "Just, be careful, okay? You don't want to run into another Dean or anything. Jerks like that are everywhere."

"Dean wasn't a jerk in the *beginning*," I said, inexplicably defending my ex as I backed down the driveway. "The money just got to him. It, like, ate his soul." Riley on the other hand…Riley was a jerk from the beginning.

"I guess so," said Meg, not sounding convinced.

"That's why I'm never letting a relationship go that far again," I said, pulling out onto Poplar Street. "But thank you *so* much for bringing up his name."

"I'm sorry! Look, I'm sure everything will work out fine. One good deed at a time, right? And this good deed should count for, like, ten regular ones." There was the sound of a door slamming in the background, followed by a small crowd cheering. "Oh, Josie, I have to go. Open mic night starts in ten minutes and the

Amazon Prime guy just got here with the mic. That was a close call! Love you!"

"Love you, too. Bye, Meg."

I shook my head as I hung up the phone. And Moose thought *I* was the loopy one.

* * *

TWO MORE DAYS had gone by, and I'd still managed to avoid running into Riley. I was sitting in my living room on Wednesday night, watching *Supernatural*, when the doorbell rang. Pixie started barking like crazy as my phone buzzed an alert from the camera by the front door. I looked at my phone, half-expecting to find Riley out there (and hating myself for the feelings that thought had stirred up). Instead, there was a mob of people.

But not just any mob.

It was my *family*. Mom, Dad, Granny, my cousin Audrey and her husband Randy, Uncle Burt and Aunt Carla; they were all standing outside on my front porch. I hadn't pushed the speaker button, but it looked to me like they were arguing. Meg was noticeably absent from the mob, and I knew right then that she must've called my parents and told them all about my dinner. I should have known from the tone of her voice how worried she'd actually been. So, she'd told them and then…what? They'd all come up here to *help*? How could that group of people out there possibly make this situation *better*?

The doorbell rang again. Oh, dear. It was probably too late to turn off all the lights and pretend I wasn't home, and I couldn't just leave them out there. Never mind that Pixie would bark herself to death if I didn't do something soon. I walked over, opened the door a crack, and peeked outside. At the sound of the door opening, all of the talking and arguing ceased, and all seven heads turned my way.

"Hi," I said, only my eyeball visible through the crack in the door.

"Josie!" said Mom, pushing the door the rest of the way open and bumping me in the forehead. "Thank goodness! For a minute I thought we might have to get a room at some horrid motel!" She pushed past me into the house, dropping a large Louis Vuitton duffle bag onto the floor.

"Hi, sweetheart," said Dad, stepping up and giving me a hug. "Sorry to surprise you like this, but Meg said you'd tell us not to come if we called ahead! As soon as I'd heard about the pickle you'd gotten yourself into, I knew we had to come up and help. I hope that's okay?"

He looked concerned, but at the same time, so *happy* at the idea of being able to help. He looked so opposite the bored man I'd seen walking up and down the beach with his metal detector these past few years, that I couldn't possibly say no. Not to him.

"Of course, it's okay," I said, hugging him back. "But Thanksgiving isn't for a week and a half!"

"I know," he said. "But we missed you! And it's not like we had anything better to do back home..."

"Fair enough. But why are *they* here?" I motioned to Uncle Burt and Aunt Carla who were still standing on the porch. Uncle Burt was holding his phone sideways, snapping photos of my house.

"Since we're staying through Thanksgiving, we had to invite them along. Couldn't let family be alone for the holiday, right?" He nudged me with his elbow. "Don't worry, they've all agreed to pitch in. You know how the saying goes: you can never have too many cooks in the kitchen!"

"That's not how the saying—"

"Holy *schnikes*!"

We both turned to look at Uncle Burt.

"Have you *seen* the Zestimate on this place?" He turned his phone to Aunt Carla, whose eyes bugged out of her head.

"Are you looking up my house on *Zillow*?"

"It's public information!" he said, pushing past us into the house. Audrey and Randy grunted their hellos, trailing behind.

"Hello, Granny," I said, turning my attention to my poor grandmother, who was still waiting patiently to be let into the house. I bent down to give her a kiss on the cheek. "Let's get you inside where it's warm!"

"This hotel is enormous!" she said, her eyes wide as she entered the house.

Hotel. Granny's words gave me the tiniest inkling of an idea. No. I *couldn't.* Could I?

"Book that spaceship to Mars yet?" called Uncle Burt, letting out a loud guffaw from somewhere inside.

Well, maybe…

"Oh, I almost forgot!" said Mom, stepping back outside onto the porch. She leaned over the railing and yelled, "Boys! She's home! You can come on up now!"

"Boys?" I gaped at her. She *didn't.*

A car door slammed and suddenly Quinn and Dylan—two of the floppy-haired dudes from last Thanksgiving—were tromping up my front steps. She *did.* They were both wearing headphones and carrying backpacks and duffle bags.

"What's up?" they said in unison, filing past me into the house and dropping their things all over the floor.

"Anybody else out there?" I asked. "Rita Winchester's son?"

"Oh, *now* you're interested," Mom groaned. "Well, it's too late, Josephine. We've already lost him. That Sophie Kilroy snatched him right up the day after we spoke on the phone. They ran into each other at The Christmas Tree Shops, of all places. What was he even *doing* there? A plastic surgeon! Anyway, I offered these two a free stay up in the mountains and they jumped at the chance. Dylan hasn't stopped talking about you since last Thanksgiving. They're both still single, if you can believe it! Brady's off the market, unfortunately. Although, between you and me"—she leaned in close, as if sharing a secret—"those hands aren't as gentle as they used to be."

"I can't believe you invited them here without even asking!" I whispered, pulling her out onto the front porch and closing the door behind us. "How many times do I have to tell you to stop trying to fix me up?"

"It's not like that at *all*," said Mom. "I just happened to be talking to them—"

"To your golf teacher and your pool boy? In November?"

Mom ignored me. "And they each said that they had no plans for Thanksgiving. Dylan's family went on a cruise, but he gets terribly seasick and had to stay behind, poor thing. And Quinn, his parents do *not* get along, so they don't even attempt to get the family together anymore."

"Oh. Well, that is sort of sad…"

"Isn't that what this dinner of yours is all about?" she asked. "Providing for people with no other place to go."

"Well, yes…"

"And sure, the fact that you didn't give either of them a chance last year didn't *completely* slip past me. Just keep an open mind! You'll have plenty of time to get to know them while they're here, and if something should happen…"

"I knew it," I said, pointing my finger at my mother and shaking my head. I turned and walked back inside with Mom hot on my heels.

"I thought it might be fun to do a *Bachelorette* sort of a thing," she said. "Do you know if they sell roses at that mini mart? It looked a little lowbrow, but maybe—"

"I'm already seeing someone!" I blurted out, as soon as I'd closed the door behind us. The words were out of my mouth before I could even think.

Everyone in the kitchen turned to look at me. Audrey and Randy, who'd already pulled a platter of cheese and crackers out of the fridge, stopped mid-bite to stare at me.

"What?" said Mom.

"I'm…I'm already seeing someone," I repeated. Then I held my chin up high and took a deep breath. "I have a boyfriend."

"You have a *boyfriend*?" asked Audrey, a wicked grin spreading across her face. "Did you confiscate his passport yet?" Randy snort-laughed.

"*No*," I said, giving her a dirty look. "It's not like that this time. This man would never hurt me. He'd never use me for my money, and he'd *never* let the money come between us. I totally and completely trust him."

I practically choked on the words as an image came to mind of the only person in town who could play the part. Even if he was the opposite of everything I'd just blathered on about. What had I done?

Mom's eyes lit up. "Well, why didn't you tell us this before, Josie? You didn't mention a word of this on the phone! What's his name?" Her face fell for a split second. "It's not *Tom*, is it?"

"No. His name is…Riley. Riley Parker. And I think—" I paused to swallow down a small geyser of stomach acid. "I think he's the one."

CHAPTER 12

I sped past the *Welcome to Summerboro* sign and in the direction of Riley's apartment. I'd ordered pizza for my family and the floppy-haired duo, and told them that I just remembered I had to check on something back at the store. I hadn't even thought to call or text Riley ahead—not that I'd have known what to say—so there I was, winging it and praying he was home. Where would Riley even go at night? He had a few friends from high school that he hung around with occasionally, but it was a Wednesday night. He could always be out at some sort of Pokémon Go evening event, since he was so in love with that game. Wouldn't that just be the kicker. No, he *had* to be home; I needed him.

As I drove, I made a mental list of any other guys I knew that might have fake boyfriend potential. There weren't many. Lee was too young. Moose was too old (and hated me). There was Mike, from The Autumnboro House of Pizza, and Nick and Tony, who were baristas at The Shaky Maple. The thing was, I couldn't ask this favor of just *anybody*. Who knew what they'd expect in return? At least with Riley, I knew exactly what he wanted, and it was innocent enough. Even if it had nearly broken my heart.

I turned onto Beach Street and parked in front of his building —a large, white Victorian that had been split into several apartments, not too different from the home he'd grown up in—and saw his black Honda Civic parked in the small lot. Thank goodness. I'd given Riley a ride home once, last summer, so I knew where he lived, but not which apartment. I knocked on the first door that I came to, which was not Riley's, but the kind man in his bathrobe directed me upstairs to unit four. I pounded on the door until I heard footsteps, and the bolt flipping.

"Moneybags," said Riley, pulling open the door. He glanced past me, to see if I was alone, and then back at my face. "What are you doing here?"

It was only seven o'clock, but he seemed to already be in his pajamas, which consisted of gray sweatpants and a T-shirt that said, *All My Friends Are Pokémon*. Without answering, I pushed past him into his apartment, ignoring the butterflies in my stomach as we briefly made contact. Apparently, they hadn't gotten the memo.

I stopped in the middle of the living room. An episode of *The Umbrella Academy* was paused on the television, with a bag of Flavor Blasted Goldfish and a bottle of Sam's OctoberFest on the coffee table. On the wall behind the couch was a gorgeous canvas print of the Tokyo skyline at night. I stared at it, mesmerized, for a few seconds, before turning around to face him.

"I want to make a deal," I said.

"A deal?" He'd closed the door, but was still standing right in front of it with one hand on the doorknob. My presence seemed to have completely thrown off his comfortable evening. Now he knew how I'd felt.

"I'm still mad at you for buttering me up," I said pointedly. "And I will probably never forgive you for that. But right now, I need your help."

Still keeping his eyes on my face, Riley walked past me into the kitchen and pulled out a chair at the small table. We sat down across from each other, and I felt for a moment what it was like to be one of his clients. How on Earth could they concentrate on such morbid subject matter with those eyes on them? Riley's eyes were made for planning weddings, not funerals.

Focus, Josie.

I cleared my throat. "I need you to be my fake boyfriend for the next week and a half."

His eyebrows lifted. "Excuse me?"

I removed my hand from where it had been partially covering my mouth, and said it again, louder. "I need you to be my *fake boyfriend* for the next week and a half."

"Your *what?*"

Oh, for Pete's sake. Had he never read a romance novel?

"My whole family showed up tonight because my sister went and blabbed about my Thanksgiving dinner," I explained. "Now my dad's all worried about me and he wants to help, which is fine, but he brought along my aunt, uncle, and cousins, which is less fine. On top of that, my mom brought along these two guys who want to marry me for my money, and she thinks I'm going to, like, *choose* one by Black Friday."

"Oh."

"Yeah. And then, I went and blurted out in front of everybody that I was already dating someone, and that it was pretty serious."

"Oops."

"Yeah, *oops.*" I rubbed my jaw. "If I have to tell them I made the whole thing up, I'll never live it down."

Riley nodded and clicked his tongue. "Are you finished?"

"I think so."

He stood up and walked to the refrigerator.

"So?" I said. "Will you do it?"

"Will I be your fake boyfriend?"

"Yes."

"Of *course* not." He pulled open the refrigerator and started taking out boxes of lunch meat.

"What do you mean *of course not?*" I jumped up and marched over, standing beside him at the kitchen counter. I tried to make eye contact, but he just kept staring down at a pack of bologna. I waved my hand in front of his face. "Hello?"

"I mean *no*. You think I'm going to…what? Go out to dinner with your family? Hold hands and talk about how we met? Speaking of which, have you met me? I don't *do* this sort of thing. It's insane."

"Of course, it's insane! But, have a heart, Riley! I need to get my mother off my case. It wouldn't even have to be the way you said." At the mention of holding hands, the butterflies in my stomach had returned in full force. The thought clearly hadn't had the same effect on Riley, as he was digging full steam ahead into his package of Oscar Meyer. "I mean, it would have to be a *little* bit like you said. But just enough for them to buy that we're a couple. Believe me, cozying up to you isn't exactly high up there on my bucket list."

"You have millions of dollars, Josie. Why don't you just hire an actor to play the part?" Without looking up, he reached for a bag of bread and started slapping together a sandwich.

An actor? I hadn't even thought of that. I shook my head. No, I didn't have the *time* for that. I needed someone now, *tonight*, before my mother broke out the roses and invited Chris Harrison over to the house.

"You know, you have some nerve," I said, stomping back into the living room.

He finally put the sandwich down and turned around. "I have some nerve?"

"Yes, you do. You tried to get all friendly with me last week, just so I would give you money. Now I ask you for one tiny favor, and you say *no?*"

"You said no to me, too, in case you forgot."

"You do realize you haven't even asked what my end of this deal would be?"

He paused, then picked up his plate and carried it into the living room, keeping his eyes on me as he sank down onto the couch. "Okay. I'll bite."

"Picture it," I said, motioning to an imaginary map above our heads. "Flying to Japan, then to China, then to Spain, Italy, France. All while seeking out those elusive little pocket monsters."

Riley took a bite of his sandwich, chewing slowly. "How do you know all that?"

I shrugged. "I did some research while I was avoiding you all week. It sounds like a pretty incredible, once-in-a-lifetime sort of a trip." It really did. I almost couldn't blame him for buttering me up. Almost.

"Okay…"

"It sounds incredible enough," I continued, sitting down on the other end of the couch, "that you should be willing to keep on pretending to like me for a measly week and a half. All you have to do is keep on doing what you were doing, and everything will work out great. I mean, I almost fell for the act; there's no reason why my family won't. As soon as they're gone, I'll tell them that we broke up and I'll write you a big, fat check."

"Josie, I wasn't pretending to like you, I—"

"Whatever," I said, cutting him off. "It's fine. It's actually great, because now I *know* what a great actor you are. I have faith in you, Riley Parker. You put on a convincing show for my family, and I give you the money for your trip. What do you say? Deal?"

He put his plate down on the coffee table and sank back into the pillows, staring up at the ceiling. I could practically see the Pikachus and Charmanders floating around inside his head.

"Okay, fine," he said, at last meeting my eyes. "What do I need to do?"

"Thank you!" I squealed. I almost leaned over to hug him, but stopped myself. Then I realized that if we were going to be pretend boyfriend and girlfriend, we were actually going to *have* to touch each other which, despite everything, still made my head feel a bit woozy. I'd just have to cross that bridge when I came to it. Instead, I reached over and tugged on the front of his Pokémon T-shirt. "I can't have my mother thinking I'm dating a twelve-year-old. What else do you have?"

"Seriously?"

"*Seriously.* Take me to your closet."

"Right this way, Moneybags," he said, standing up and guiding me toward the bedroom.

Riley and me, walking toward his bedroom. No big deal. I tried to remind myself that we were only going in there to look inside his closet, and that he was only interested in my money, but that didn't seem to help my sweaty palms. I stepped into the room, making note of the rumpled gray sheets on the queen-sized bed, the warm glow of the lamp on the nightstand. The framed *Back to the Future* movie poster on the wall and the piles of dirty laundry scattered around the floor. The room was small, and a bit messy, but it wouldn't be the worst place in the world to wake up. I shook away the image that came to mind and turned to face the closet. We had some work to do.

CHAPTER 13

"*I* look ridiculous," said Riley.

After inspecting his entire wardrobe, I'd decided it was probably best if he just put one of his funeral planning suits back on. We were now at my house, parked at the end of the driveway behind all the other cars. Neither of us was quite ready to get out of the car yet.

"You wear that suit to work all the time," I said. "What's the problem?"

"I wear suits to *work*. Why would I possibly still be wearing one now?"

"Maybe because you were working late? Or because you're a sophisticated, classy guy who loves wearing suits? Maybe you've never worn a hooded sweatshirt in your life. Maybe you don't even have a Pokémon Go addiction. Which reminds me, you need to leave your phone in the car."

"No way!"

"Yes way! I can't have you staring at that thing all night. I need you to look like you can't take your eyes off of *me*, not that thing." I motioned to the phone that he was cradling in his hands like a security blanket. He glared at me until I started humming the Pokémon theme song. *Gotta catch 'em all!*

"Fine." In a huff, he handed me the phone and I put it in the glove compartment.

"Great. Let's go."

I walked around the car to meet him on the passenger side, almost laughing when I saw the expression on his face.

"You *cannot* go in and meet my family looking like you're about to throw up," I said. "What's wrong with you?"

"Give me a break! I'm nervous. You do realize what we're doing isn't normal, right?"

"Oh, come on, what happened to those great acting skills you used on me and Catrina? I know you can turn it on when you want something. And right now, I know you want my money."

Riley shook his head. "For my fake girlfriend, you really don't know me at all."

"Just do your best," I said, sticking out my hand.

I tried to appear unaffected as he reached out and took it, but inside I was melting. I'd imagined a lot of scenarios between the two of us over the summer—most of them involving much more than just innocent hand-holding—but this was better than anything I'd pictured. Riley's real-life hand, holding mine. Even if it was totally fake and all for show, physical contact was physical contact. I took a step closer and looked up at his face. He still looked ill.

"You'll be fine," I said gently, giving his hand a squeeze. "Just be yourself."

He gave me a small smile, and we continued on our way up the driveway. Pixie was already barking like a maniac at my arrival. I quickly unlocked the front door and she ran straight at me, running circles around my legs.

"Hello!" I said to Pixie, crouching down to pet her. "I missed you too! Who's a good girl? Who's a good girl? Oh, yes!" When she'd finally settled down, I stood up to find Mom and Dad standing in the front hall, staring at us. I gave Riley's hand a squeeze.

"Mom, Dad, this is my boyfriend…Riley."

Mom stepped forward first, seeming to inspect him from all sides, as if to make sure he was real and not some sort of hologram I'd paid thousands of dollars for (hadn't thought of that). Dad was looking at him with his *If you hurt my daughter, I'll kill you* face that I recognized from the first time he'd met Dean. That look might be part of the reason Dean decided to run off to another continent, now that I think about it.

I slipped my arm around Riley's waist, sending out telepathic messages. *Please relax. Please look like you love me.* When he didn't move, I gave his waist a hard squeeze. Finally, he stuck his hand out.

"It's nice to meet you, Mr. Morgan. Mrs. Morgan." He shook with both of my parents, before stuffing his hand back into his pocket.

"It's lovely to meet you, too," said Mom. "I have to confess, this is quite the surprise. Josie never even mentioned that she was seeing anybody!"

"Well, it all happened so fast," I said. "The way we fell in love. Isn't that right, honey?"

"Mm hmm," said Riley. I gave him another moment to elaborate, but that seemed to be all we were getting.

"I used to bring Riley coffee at his work *all* summer," I continued, "but he didn't realize how he felt about me until he saw me trick-or-treating with another man this past Halloween."

"You still go trick-or-treating?" asked Audrey, appearing from the kitchen. "That is so lame."

"It's an Autumnboro tradition!" I said. "All the adults do it!" Okay, so maybe I wasn't the greatest at making up convincing lies on the spot.

"Anyway," I went on, trying to focus only on my parents, "after he saw me swapping Snickers bars with this other man, he was so overcome with jealousy that he spelled out my name in pumpkins across the town common! It was so magical!"

"That is so romantic," said Mom, her eyes misting over as she looked up at Riley. "And what is it that you do for work? If I had to guess by the suit, I'd say…financial planner?"

"Funeral planner," he said, bobbing his head up and down. "I plan funerals."

"Oh," said Mom, her face falling.

"I'd be happy to plan yours," he said, motioning to her and Dad. "Josie hasn't let me plan hers yet, but I'll talk her into it, eventually." He gave me a wink. I pinched his waist, hard.

"That's…lovely," said Mom, taking a step back. "But I think we're all set with, um, with our funerals." She cleared her throat and gave Dad a push forward.

"Carter Morgan," he said, stepping up and shaking Riley's hand again. "Geography teacher, thirty-two years. What's the capital of Maryland?"

"Um, Annapolis?"

Dad clapped Riley on the shoulder and smiled at me, the murderous look gone from his eyes. "Whatever he does for a living, I like this one. Dean said *Baltimore*. Idiot." He walked into the living room and sat down on the couch.

At the mention of my ex, Riley looked down at me quizzically. I shook my head. I wasn't planning on getting into any of *that* right now. "Come on, let's go meet everybody else."

Mom and Pixie followed us into the living room, where there were pizza boxes and greasy paper plates covering every surface. Pixie snatched up a piece of crust that had fallen onto the carpet. A bottle of very expensive champagne was open on the coffee table, and Uncle Burt had his dirty shoes up on the back of my furry black bear footstool. There was a football game on the television, and Randy was flipping through a magazine that I was pretty sure I'd left upstairs in the master bathroom. *Breathe, Josie.*

At the sight of us walking into the room, Dylan and Quinn

both stood from their places on the couch, drawing themselves up to their full heights. I rolled my eyes as they sized up Riley, who looked like a million bucks in his suit. Dylan and Quinn could just take their Vineyard Vines T-shirts and stuff them where the—

"Riley Parker," said Riley, holding out his hand and shaking with both Dylan and Quinn. "I'm sorry to disappoint you, but Josephine here is off the market." He smiled at me and pulled me close. Thank goodness he seemed to be loosening up.

"That's not what Shelly told us," said Quinn, nodding toward my mother.

"Well, *Shelly* was a little behind the times," I said. "But now we're all caught up! Come on, honey." I pulled Riley along to where Granny was sitting in the recliner.

"Granny, this is my boyfriend." I crouched down in front of her. "This is Riley."

"Hello, dear," she said, resting a magazine in her lap and reaching up her hand. Riley crouched down in front of her, as well, so she could pat his cheek. "You're going to love this hotel!"

"I always stay here when I'm in town," he said. "You have very good taste." Granny batted a hand at him, looking smitten.

"So, you're the new guy, huh?" asked Uncle Burt, looking up from the TV. "*The one?*"

"That's what she tells me," said Riley, turning around.

"And you know all about the money?" asked Aunt Carla.

"I know all about it," said Riley. "Josie does a lot of good, and helps a lot of people with that money. That's one of the things I love about her."

My breath caught at his words. It seemed that he'd found his acting skills after all.

"Lucky them," said Aunt Carla. "Because she's super stingy with *us.* I haven't seen a single check since Christmas."

"Me neither," chimed in Randy.

"That's because you blew it on an RV!" I said. "And you two blew yours at the casino!"

"At least we had some *fun* with it," said Randy. "This one, she spends it on high school fundraisers and mosquito nets."

"Malaria is no laughing matter! Just five dollars' worth of mosquito nets can save—"

"And don't even think about asking her to pay for your gastric bypass," interrupted Uncle Burt, leaning back against the couch and adjusting his belt buckle.

"So, Riley, how do you feel about Thailand?" asked Audrey.

"Can we please change the subject?" I asked, trying to move Riley along again, but this time, he wouldn't budge. That's when I noticed the look on his face. It was…intense. Angry, almost.

"Josie's handling that money better than anybody I could possibly imagine," he said slowly, looking from Burt to Carla. "Whatever she's given to you was out of the goodness of her heart, because she's the kindest person I know. But she doesn't *owe* you anything."

Woah. That…that didn't seem like part of the act. And when he turned to look from them to me, his eyes were filled with so much heat that I was caught completely off guard. Before any of us could respond, an all too familiar sound came from Quinn's phone, and Riley's head swiveled around.

"Is that Pokémon Go?" he asked, his little stint at being chivalrous apparently over.

"Yeah," said Quinn, tapping at the screen. "Josie's got a *ton* of good ones in her house. You should see what I just got."

Before Riley's head could do a full three-sixty, I dragged him away from Quinn's phone and over to the love seat, where I forced him to sit. I angled myself toward him and whispered into his ear, "Don't even *think* about it."

"Think about what?" he whispered back.

"That stupid game," I said, resting my left hand on his right leg so it looked like we were whispering sweet romantic sentiments to each other. "You can play it when you get home." My hair brushed against his face, making me aware of how close we were. I felt his thigh muscles twitch beneath my hand, and I gave his knee a squeeze. We settled back into the couch, still shoulder-to-shoulder.

"Josie, dear, did you ever speak to that Dean again?" asked Granny, out of the blue.

"What?" My body, which had been slowly sinking into Riley, immediately tensed up.

"Did you ever speak to *Dean* again?" she repeated. "After he took your money and abandoned you in Australia?"

Audrey let out a loud snort from across the room, as I felt my cheeks starting to burn. Okay, so maybe I hadn't given Amy the *entire* humiliating story. Leave it to Granny to choose now to have one of her rare moments of clarity. Without looking, I felt Riley's eyes on me.

"No, Granny," I said, blinking back sudden tears. "I never did."

"That's a shame," she went on, dreamily. "You were so in love. You even thought he was going to propose!"

The room went silent, and Granny went back to flipping through her magazine—already back to happily thinking she was staying at the Ritz. I suddenly felt Riley's arm, warm and heavy, around my shoulders.

"Dean was a moron," he said matter-of-factly, as if he actually knew anything in the world about him. Then he kissed me softly on the top of the head.

CHAPTER 14

⤬

*J*put Riley through another hour of socializing with my family—Audrey suddenly had a photographic memory of every family get-together Dean ever attended—before announcing that I was taking him home. Riley looked almost as excited as Pixie as the two of them dove into my car.

"I'm sorry about all that," I said, as he fastened his seatbelt. "My dad and Granny, they're the normal ones. The rest of them —" I shook my head and started backing down the driveway. "Ghouls."

"You don't have to apologize," said Riley, loosening his tie and unbuttoning the top two buttons of his shirt. "But why do you let them talk to you like that?"

"I tried to defend myself," I said. "You heard me. They just don't get it. Not that it's completely their fault. Yes, my family's gone nuts, but *I'm* the one that brought all this money into their lives."

"I'm pretty sure your aunt and uncle were jerks before you won any money. No offense."

"Well, sure...but the money pushed them way over the edge. My fault."

We drove for a while in silence while Riley tapped around on my Tesla's touchscreen. "Which button makes us fly?"

"You sound like Uncle Burt," I said, rolling my eyes. "It's just a *car.*" I put on my right turn signal, making a fart sound come out of Riley's seat.

"What the—"

"*Geez*, Riley. Couldn't wait until you got home?"

"Not funny."

"It's actually *very* funny."

I chuckled some more as he went back to tapping at the touchscreen. Finally, he found the setting for fart mode and turned it off.

"Romance mode?" he asked, noticing the other unique settings I had available.

"It just, um, puts a fireplace on the screen, dims the lights… turns up the heat." I ran a hand through my hair. "You're supposed to use it when you're parked."

"Ah." He nodded, and we rode on in silence for a few more minutes.

"So," he said, just after we'd passed the *Welcome to Summerboro* sign, "I heard a lot of bits and pieces about this Dean tonight. What's the full story there?"

My stomach filled with nerves as I swung past Sweet Something, Peach's Diner, and the town lake, my thumbs drumming against the steering wheel. *What's the full story there?* Nobody outside of my family knew the entire story. Ideally, only Mom, Dad, and Meg would have ever known the truth, but then Mom went and blabbed everything to Aunt Carla over a bottle of chardonnay one night. I supposed I should tell Riley the whole story, since it was likely to come up over and over again, now that we were spending time with my über tactful family.

I took a deep breath, and began to talk. First, I told him the same things I'd told Amy—how I'd met Dean online, how I'd thought we were going to get married—right up until the point where I'd told her that he hopped a plane to Thailand. By that time, we'd arrived outside Riley's house, so I put the car into park and I finished the story.

"We were on our first big trip together," I said. "We'd just finished the first week out of a three-week trip to Australia. Everything had been going great, you know? And I'd thought, just from the way things had been going, that maybe this was *it*. I mean, we'd been dating for nearly two years, and like Granny said, I was basically waiting on him to propose. This trip...the timing...it was all so perfect." I stared out of the windshield, focusing on the stop sign at the end of the street—trying to remember what it had felt like to be so happy and in love; to think that life could only get better.

"I feel a big *but* coming," said Riley.

I turned to look at him, still embarrassed to finish, yet feeling oddly safe with just the two of us, alone, in my car. I glanced down at his left hand, resting on his leg, and I went on, "But then he was gone."

"Gone?"

I nodded as all those panicky, sick feelings returned to my stomach. That first memory of waking up and thinking he was in the bathroom, and then later that maybe he'd gone out for coffee, and then later—

"He wasn't answering his phone," I continued. "And his wallet and his passport were gone, plus all of his clothes. It was super obvious to anybody with half a brain that he'd up and ditched me, but to me...I was just worried that something *terrible* had happened to him. I told the people at the hotel, and they called in the police—who thought I was a naïve fool, too, I could tell. I mean, nobody packs a suitcase while they're being kidnapped, right? But I just didn't want to admit it." I took a deep breath. "The police, they eventually tracked his cell phone and his credit cards, and they told me that he'd flown to Bangkok. Checked into some fancy hotel...with a *guest*." I flopped my head against the back of the seat and looked at Riley. "And I thought we were coming home engaged."

"I am so sorry," he said, looking back at me, his eyes intense but warm. "I had no idea. You…you didn't deserve that."

"Ya think?" I forced a smile.

"Can I ask how much he made off with?"

I sighed and pinched the bridge of my nose. "Before I tell you, you have to remember that we were together for *two years*. And that I was young and naïve and still had faith in the human race."

"I'm not going to judge you, Josie. I was just curious. You don't have to tell me."

"No, it's fine. So, with the money for his start-up company, plus the condo I bought him—which he *sold*, unbeknownst to me, right before our trip—plus all the other gifts I'd stupidly given him over the years—which was totally against everything my financial advisor ever told me…about half a million?"

Riley groaned.

"Not that half a million made a huge dent or anything," I added. "It was more about, you know, being used."

"I'm sorry," he said again.

"And my mom, she obviously didn't learn anything from my experience. She still tries to set me up with anybody and everybody. And my relatives, I think they actually find it *funny*."

"That's when all your fears started."

I nodded. "Whenever I think about traveling, I feel so sick. It's like I'm right back there in that hotel room, or on that long flight back home, all alone. But it worked out, in a way, because as long as I stay here in Autumnboro, where it's safe, nothing bad will happen to me, and my family won't ever have to deal with the reality of having all this money. *Now* you know the reason I believe money warps people. It's because I've seen it turn a nice, decent human being into someone willing to ditch his girlfriend in Australia."

Riley's face darkened. "You realize Dean wasn't a good guy no matter *what* your financial circumstances, right?"

"That's not true..."

"It is," he said. "No nice, decent human being would've ditched you in Australia, Josie. No matter what. Dean was bad news. You were *lucky* he took half a million and ran."

"Lucky?" I laughed. "Right. That's a good one."

"You were," said Riley, fixing me with a fiery look that quickly stopped my laughter. "Even if you didn't have a dime, no way did you deserve to spend your life with a guy like that."

Oh. He looked so...offended. Almost angry that I hadn't realized this for myself. I had the sudden urge to reach over and flick on Romance Mode, but kept my hands in my lap.

"I guess I never thought of it that way," I said, softly. Was it true? Had Dean always been a jerk? I mean, Meg told me that he was, but I figured she was just trying to make me feel better after Australia. "So, um, are you around tomorrow night? If I need you?"

"Yeah," he said, looking straight ahead and blowing out a deep breath "Sure. Just tell me where to be, and I'll be there."

"Thanks, Riley. You really helped me out tonight."

"Well, I've got the trip of a lifetime on the line, so..."

"Even so." I nudged him with my elbow. "You were a better sport than I thought you'd be."

"No problem," he said, opening the door and stepping out of the car. "Have a good rest of your night with the *ghouls*." With a teasing smile, he slammed the door behind him. He was halfway to his building, when he turned around and jogged back. I held my breath as I lowered the passenger window.

"My phone?" he said, bending down and holding out his hand.

Right. I took it out of the glove compartment, noticing the three thousand game notifications on the screen. "Enjoy."

Our fingers touched as I handed him the phone—which should have been no big deal, as we'd been fake holding hands all night—but my breath caught just the same, and I wondered if maybe he'd felt something, too.

Then he was gone from my window, back to his phone. Back to his real life, where I was nothing more than a convenient source of cash for a trip of a lifetime. I was a somewhat less convenient source of cash now that I'd asked this favor of him, but he was willing enough to play along. Dean had been willing to play along, too, and for two entire *years*. At least this time, I was in on the act.

CHAPTER 15

After I returned home last night from dropping off Riley, I got straight down to the business of sleeping arrangements. I gave Granny the quietest and most comfortable of the spare bedrooms, making sure she was snugly tucked in with plenty of warm blankets, and giving her a tiny bell to ring in case she needed anything. Mom and Dad were given the second nicest spare room, with the electric fireplace and the faux bearskin rug. Audrey and Randy were relegated to the room at the back of the house, close to the tree with the howling fisher cats. Uncle Burt and Aunt Carla got the room directly over my home theater, and the floppy-haired duo were sent to sleep in the basement, where they could watch movies and play all the Xbox their hearts desired. I encouraged them to really crank up the volume as soon as they heard Uncle Burt snoring.

I was awoken at six o'clock in the morning by Uncle Burt belting out "Despacito" in the shower. His singing must have also woken up Quinn and Dylan, because I found them, soon after, in the kitchen making waffles in their underwear.

Let me rephrase that.

I found Dylan and Quinn in the kitchen using the waffle

maker I'd ordered from *In the Kitchen with David*—the one I hadn't even taken out of the box yet—to make waffles, while walking around in their boxer briefs. They'd dripped chocolate sauce, strawberries, and whipped cream all over the place, and kept flexing their pecs any time we made eye contact, which, believe me, I was keeping to a minimum. Audrey and Randy were also up early (the fisher cats had been quite vocal last night), dressed in matching bathrobes that they'd clearly stolen from a Marriott hotel. I found them flipping through a pile of credit card statements that I'd definitely left on the desk in my upstairs office. I ripped the statements out of their hands and stuffed them into my purse.

This was so not going to work.

By nine o'clock, I'd concocted a plan. Actually, the plan had been brewing in my mind ever since Granny said the word *hotel* yesterday. I had a key to The Autumnboro Inn burning a hole in my pocket, and several people that I refused to share my home with for the next week and a half. Granny, Mom, and Dad were welcome to stay here, of course. As for the rest of them? They were being relocated to the inn, whether they liked it or not. There were no personal items at the inn for them to nose through. Nobody to disturb with their singing, or their twitchy pectoral muscles, or their opinions on how I handled my finances. Nobody to disturb except for themselves. It would be glorious. Kit and Amy would never even need to find out. I'd make sure everybody was moved back into my house by Thanksgiving night, and I'd give the inn a thorough, bonus cleaning before the grand opening. It was a win-win.

The announcement was surprisingly well received. The only complaint came from Audrey and Randy, who wanted to be allowed over to my house to use the hot tub whenever they wanted. I talked them down to a maximum of three visits between the hours of five and seven p.m., and we had a deal.

I led the caravan into town, and made sure that everybody

parked in the small lot behind the inn, where their cars wouldn't be seen from the street. I couldn't have it looking like the inn was open for business or anything. I found the room keys all hanging neatly from hooks behind the front desk. It was a very old-school way of doing things, but the wall of keys had been part of Rebecca's Parker's journal drawings, and so that was the way Kit had wanted it.

I had fun handing out keys and assigning rooms, despite the nagging little voice in my head telling me to call Kit to make sure this was actually okay. I showed everybody up to their rooms, and made sure the bathrooms were stocked with towels, soaps, and tiny bottles of pumpkin spice-scented shampoo and conditioner. He hadn't asked for my opinion on a single thing having to do with this inn; he'd just taken my money and run. He *owed* me this much. I fluffed up the pillows and opened the blinds.

"I have to go over and open my store now," I said, gathering everybody back into the sitting room for a brief meeting. "So, you're on your own. There's a grocery store not too far from here, and a mini mart just up the street. Please don't break anything, or put your shoes on the furniture, or answer the phone. Just take it easy. Take a nap! Read a book!" If it was summer, or if there were snow on the ground, there would be plenty of outdoor activities they could do. But in the middle of November? Not so much.

I took one last look around. Uncle Burt had his feet up on the coffee table and was trying to turn on the television with the remote for the ceiling fan. Dylan and Quinn had wandered into the kitchen and turned on the garbage disposal. Aunt Carla was staring at the autumn-decorated Christmas tree with distaste, and poking at a scarecrow. Audrey and Randy were crouched down, peering into Tom's model stagecoach, probably trying to figure out where the batteries went.

Maybe this *was* a bad idea. Although, the alternative—everybody living in my house for a week and a half—would be even worse. No, letting my family stay here was the least Kit could do to pay me back. If I called him to ask permission, it would just stress him out when he and Amy were finally getting some time off to relax.

Besides, like Moose said, I had more money than God. There wasn't anything they could do to this place that I wouldn't be able to fix.

* * *

I'D BEEN WALKING around the store making a list of items to markdown for my Black Friday sale, when I heard a loud scuffling coming from the sidewalk outside. I was about to investigate, when the door burst open in a loud jangling of bells, and Dylan and Quinn tumbled inside.

"Hey, Josie," said Quinn, pushing himself in front of Dylan.

"Hey, Josie," said Dylan, ducking around Quinn and heading toward me, the floorboards creaking under his feet.

"Um, hey, guys," I said. "Everything going okay at the inn?"

"Of course," said Quinn. He'd darted ahead of Dylan and was now standing directly in front of me, his left elbow making a huge dent in a stack of tea towels he was leaning on. I yanked them out from under him. "I came by to take you to lunch."

"Actually, *I* came by to take you to lunch," said Dylan, who'd snuck around to my other side. He plucked a heavy cinnamon candle off the shelf and started tossing it from one hand to the other. "I was here first, but then *this* one showed up after he said he was staying home to watch *Over the Top* with your uncle. I'm willing to fight for you, Josie. You know that, right?"

"Is that what I heard outside? You two were *fighting?*"

"You're worth it," said Quinn. "I drove across three states to prove it to you."

"Massachusetts and New Hampshire are neighbors," I said, rolling my eyes and grabbing the candle out of Dylan's hand. At least it wasn't lit. "You two don't even *know* me. The only reason you came up here is because my mother told you I was rich. And I'm pretty sure I've already made it clear that I have a boyfriend."

"That guy?" said Dylan, following me over to the counter. "He was a total downer. A loser. He works at a *funeral home*."

"You clean my mother's pool."

"That's just a stepping stone! You and me, Josie, we could be a power couple someday. Just hear me out, I've got this *great* idea for an app…"

I rolled my eyes and looked over at Quinn. "Let me guess. You've got a great idea for an app too?"

"It's for matching up middle-aged women with golf instructors," he said, miming a golf swing. "The first thing they do is enter their favorite—"

"Stop!" I groaned. "Both of you! I've heard it all before, and I'm tired of it! I'm only letting you stay because my mother invited you, and I feel bad that you don't have any other Thanksgiving plans, but that's where it ends! Why don't you two take a drive to North Woodstock for lunch? There's a great brewery down there. Maybe you'll meet someone who's *actually interested*."

I picked up my phone and typed a text message to Riley. **I know it's early, but can you swing by?** I'd had enough of Dylan and Quinn, and I may as well get my money's worth out of this fake boyfriend deal. Riley almost immediately texted back a thumbs-up emoji. Thank goodness.

I put my phone down and opened my laptop. I pretended to order some inventory, while Dylan and Quinn—totally not taking the hint—continued filling me in on their various life accomplishments (Quinn inherited his dead grandma's Mercedes; Dylan once saw Nicki Minaj at the airport). I couldn't believe my mother thought I'd be better off with one of these dopes, rather than remaining single for eternity.

Less than ten minutes later, the bells jingled as Riley walked through the door. He brushed off Dylan and Quinn with a glance, before turning to me with a smile that stopped my heart. He must've been working on it during his walk over, because the act was flawless. He looked genuinely delighted to see me, as if the best part of his day was currently in progress.

"Hey, you," he said, walking behind the counter and up to my stool. With one hand on my back, he planted a kiss on the top of my head.

"Hey, *you*," I said, smiling up at him, a bit stunned. The place where his lips had been felt all tingly. I hadn't been expecting that, though I couldn't complain. I reached out and took his hand, lifted it to my lips, and planted a kiss on the back. If everything were different, I could definitely get used to this. "Ready for lunch?"

"Ready."

"Okay, everybody out!" I said, with renewed determination. I slid off my stool, grabbed my coat, and started shepherding a grumbling Dylan and Quinn toward the door.

"After you," said Riley, fixing each of them with an intense stare until they'd exited ahead of him. As soon as I'd locked the door behind us, he picked up a large shovel that had been leaning against the building, and hefted it over his shoulder. Several clumps of grass and dirt fell to the ground.

I raised my eyebrows. "What's *that* for?"

"I felt like digging a few graves after lunch," he said, looking from me, to Dylan and Quinn. Their eyes widened as they took several steps back, then they both turned and hurried off down the sidewalk.

"See you guys later!" I called after them, waving. They didn't turn around. Once they were out of earshot, I turned back to Riley. "You're a gravedigger now?"

He leaned the shovel back against the building. "Nah, one of the DPW guys must have left this here. I saw it before I came in."

"You're an evil genius." I laughed, giving him a playful push in the stomach. "I have the best fake boyfriend ever."

He gave me another of those heart-stopping smiles, before looking up at the *Gobble 'til We Wobble!* flag outside The Plaid Apple. "Did you really want to grab lunch? Or was that just part of the act?"

"I could eat," I said, not wanting him to go back to work just yet. "You?"

"Sure," he said. "Let's do it."

CHAPTER 16

*L*et's do it.

Sigh.

There were a few annoying parts of my body that didn't seem to understand he was only talking about eating *lunch*. Or maybe they were so desperate that they didn't even care. I tried to calm my racing heart as we walked into The Plaid Apple. Even though it was lunchtime, the restaurant wasn't very busy. Riley and I were able to grab the best booth in the house—the one by the windows, with the cleanest tabletop and the least number of rips in the upholstery. Amy liked to say that The Plaid Apple's tattered décor only added to its charm and character. I just wanted to slip Jackie some cash so she could finally redecorate, but I had a feeling she wouldn't take too kindly to that idea. Despite its outdated furnishings, the restaurant was always cozy and welcoming, and smelled like freshly baked apple pies, so I couldn't really complain. Moose, as usual, was having lunch at the counter, sipping coffee and talking to Jackie.

"So, do you think those two got the hint?" asked Riley. He pushed aside the red café curtains to look out the window.

"Well, I don't know if they've given up on *me*," I said. "But you certainly scared them away from ever dating *you*." I chuckled as I flipped through a menu, still picturing the expressions on their faces when they'd seen that shovel.

"Why don't you just send them back home?" he asked. "They're really staying at your house with your relatives? That's a little weird."

I bit my lip and looked up at him sheepishly. "Actually…I may have moved some of them over to the inn."

"The *inn*?" He laid his menu down on the table and stared at me. "As in, my brother's inn?"

"Please don't tell him," I begged. "It'll be fine, I swear! He'll never even know they were there."

Riley shook his head and picked his menu up again. "Being your fake boyfriend is about all I can handle. I'm staying out of this."

"Thank you," I said. "Besides, you met my relatives. It's not like you can blame me."

"You do make a good point."

"So," I said, after we'd looked over our menus for a few minutes, "I was thinking, if we're going to be fake boyfriend and girlfriend, I should probably know a few personal details about you."

I looked up to find Riley staring at his phone. He had it pointed at the corner of the restaurant and was tapping away at Pokéballs. "Riley?"

"Huh?"

"I said if we're going to be fake boyfriend and girlfriend, I should probably know a few personal details about you."

"Oh, right. Sorry." He laid his phone down on the table and focused his attention on me. "What do you want to know?"

Before I could answer, Jackie came by to take our order.

"Cute shirt," I said. It was a pale pink T-shirt with a picture of a raccoon hanging from a tree branch. The words *Hanging Out at Clark's Trading Post* were stretched tightly across her chest.

"Thanks, hon," said Jackie. "And I just love your top. Isaac Mizrahi?"

"You know it. Do you want one? I have ten at home, all sizes and colors. It was such a good deal, and Amy's mom said it was the only order of the season. I know she always says that's a total lie, but better safe than sorry, right?"

Moose, who had been eavesdropping from his seat at the counter, let out a loud snort. He always did that when I mentioned finding a good deal. The annoying thing was that he'd snort that exact same way if I were bragging about blowing tons of money on a fancy sports car. I couldn't win with him.

"Hi, Moose!" I said, leaning around Jackie and giving him a bright smile. "I met your nephew the other day. Lee?"

He spun slowly around on his stool to face me. "Oh, yeah?"

"Yup. Great kid. *Really* good at his job at the newspaper, but I'm trying to convince him to give college a chance. He said that you really wanted him to go, which I think is *so* sweet."

Moose's eyes narrowed as he took a long sip from his coffee mug. I could almost hear the gears in his head turning, trying to reconcile the size of my bank account with the fact that I was possibly a decent human being. He nodded, grunted, and turned back to his lunch. I called that progress.

"She's such a doll," said Jackie, nudging my shoulder. "Isn't she a doll?" She looked over at Riley, who was staring at me with an amused expression on his face. An expression that Jackie must have mistaken for something else, because her eyes suddenly lit up.

"Hang on a minute…are you two…" She motioned back and forth between us while waggling her eyebrows.

"We are," I said, giving Riley a helpless look. Apparently, the entire town was about to think we were dating. "Riley and I…are a couple."

"I *knew* it," she said, slapping her notepad down on the table and making our silverware jump. "Ever since last Halloween when you did that group costume, I said *those* two would make a perfect couple. Hey, everybody!" She turned to face the restaurant. "Josie and Riley are a couple!" A few people clapped and whistled, while Riley's face turned as red as the apple décor.

"I think we're ready to order now," I said, smiling up at Jackie as I gently tapped Riley's foot beneath the table. "Sorry about that," I whispered, after she'd left.

"I knew what I was signing up for," he said. "Sort of."

I smiled. "I'm sure it'll be worth the humiliation once we've 'broken up' and you're off on your trip, seeing the world." I felt a small pang of jealousy at the thought of all the cool places he was going to see. There was that funny thought again—*me*, jealous. I could go anywhere I wanted to if I didn't have my very valid reasons for staying home. I cleared my throat. "So, you were about to tell me some juicy stuff about yourself?"

He leaned back against the seat, his fingers drumming on the table. "I'm not really good at the whole 'tell me about yourself' thing."

"Oh," I said. "Okay. Well, how about I ask questions and you answer them?"

"Fire away."

Hmm. I'd taken Riley's lack of conversation so personally all summer. Had I ever even bothered to ask him anything about himself? I've always been so chatty and ready to offer up info about myself without *needing* to be asked, that it hadn't occurred to me he might not be the same way.

"Well?"

"Sorry," I said, shaking my head. "Okay, so, um...let's start with college. You went to...?"

"UNH."

"For?"

"Business."

"And you ended up as a funeral planner...how?"

Riley squinted one eye. "Do you want the long answer or the short answer?"

"What's the short answer?"

"That I came back to Autumnboro after college, there was a job opening at the funeral home, and I took it."

"And the long one?"

"All right." He sighed, resting his elbows on the table and folding his hands in front of his chin. He really did have the jawline of a Greek god. I looked away and took a sip of ice water. Counted the apples on the wallpaper until he started to speak. "After my mom died, back in high school, I became a little...odd."

"Odder than you are now?"

"Oh, yeah. My dad had already left, when I was a baby. Kit was depressed and miserable to be around. Amy took off for college without even saying goodbye. I had some abandonment issues going on, for sure. My grandmother, she did the best she could, but I could tell she was having a rough time. First, she had to handle all the funeral arrangements, then she had to basically tie up my mom's entire life that had been left hanging. Never mind that she was suddenly responsible for raising two teenagers. Our mom hadn't made *any* sort of preparations, you know? Nobody ever expects to die young."

I nodded. Amy had told me all about what happened after Kit and Riley's mom passed away that summer. Riley had been so young; it broke my heart thinking of what he'd gone through without much of a support system. If only I'd known him back then.

"Anyway," he continued, "I ended up going full-on, cliché goth kid. Black clothes, dyed hair...*eyeliner.*"

I whistled. "Sexy."

"Right." He laughed. "Thankfully, by the time I went to college, I'd outgrown most of that. I got my business degree, and then I came back here. Figured I'd work in a bank or something. But when I saw the job opening at Goldwyn & Hays, it just made sense to me. I could help people to prepare for everything my family hadn't been prepared for. It's not morbid, like everybody thinks. To me, it's just…selfless." He shrugged. "That's all I've got."

"That's more than enough," I said, my heart melting as I reached across the table for his hand. He looked me in the eyes for a moment, before letting me take it. I knew we wouldn't even be here right now if it weren't for the fact that Riley needed money…but still. "I just wish you'd told me all that before."

"It's not really the sort of thing you bring up over Pokémon Go."

"No." I chuckled, squeezing his hand. "I guess what I meant was, I wish I'd *asked* you about all that before. You gave your sad story a happy ending. I like that."

He smiled and gently rubbed the top of my hand with his thumb, sending a tingle all the way up my arm. Jackie smiled at us from behind the counter.

"Hopefully getting a job at a funeral home isn't the *actual* ending to my story," he said.

"You know what I mean."

He's sweet, but he's still after your money, Josie. They all are. It was a nice try, but the little voice in my head wasn't enough to make me pull my hand away. We stayed like that for a few more seconds, until Jackie came over to deliver our food—and to tell us how adorable we looked.

"One more question," I said, squirting ketchup onto my plate. "How'd you end up so addicted to that phone?"

Riley shrugged. "You can add social anxiety to my list of issues. Having my phone in my hand has always sort of just… helped. It gives me something to focus on. I can't really explain it. I wouldn't say I'm the only one." He motioned to the other people in the restaurant, half of whom were staring down at their phones.

Riley had social anxiety. That didn't excuse all the buttering up he'd been doing before asking me for money, but it did make me see our interactions over the summer in a different light. The way he'd invite me out on walks and then spend the entire time looking at his phone. Maybe he hadn't been bored, or annoyed with me…maybe I'd just made him nervous.

"Speaking of phones," he said, putting his burger down on the plate and picking up his phone, "I saw something this morning, and I thought of you. You should sell these at the store."

He slid it across the table. On the screen was a picture of a dog who looked just like Pixie, dressed in the most gorgeous autumn sweater. It was chunky knit with stripes of crimson and gold, with little pumpkin pom-poms.

"Aw, I love it!" I said, making note of the website so I could order some as soon as I got back to the store. I was going to make this Etsy shop owner's week.

"I had a feeling you would," he said, going back to his fries. He glanced up at me one more time, though, while I was still looking down at his phone. He probably thought I hadn't noticed, but I did. The way he'd looked at me, I felt it all the way down to my toes. Self-conscious, I slid the phone back across the table and tried to focus on my lunch. Jawline of a Greek god, and a heart of gold to boot. Now he was picking out sweaters for my dog.

None of this was helping my crush in the slightest. None of it. Not. One. Tiny. Bit.

CHAPTER 17

*S*everal hours later, and I was still on a bit of a high from my lunch with Riley. Or maybe it was from the two Maple Sugar Crushes we'd grabbed before heading back to work. As soon as I'd returned to my store, I ordered ten of those adorable dog sweaters, then spent some time chatting away with customers and working on my window display. Last week, I'd set up a scene of Pilgrim teddy bears having Thanksgiving dinner around a long, rustic wooden bench that I'd found at the Summerboro flea market. Arranged on the bench was a very realistic, but fake, roast turkey and stuffing (that cost more than I'd ever admit to Moose), pumpkin-shaped stoneware mugs, and flickering, flameless candles in shades of cranberry and caramel. Long garlands of autumn leaves, mixed with fairy lights, hung straight down from above. I loved Pumpkin Everything, and I had from the very first time I stepped through its door.

It was the first weekend after I moved to Autumnboro. With nothing else to do, I'd taken a drive over to Main Street to have a look around. Its lovely town center had been one of the main reasons I'd chosen Autumnboro in the first place, but I'd yet to actually go inside any of its shops. Pumpkin Everything was the first one I chose, and it was there that I'd found an old man seated behind the counter, staring perplexedly at his cell phone. I introduced myself, and spent the next hour helping Tom set up the new smartphone that his daughter had sent him in the mail.

It turned out that we had a lot in common—I'd been recently dumped by my boyfriend and didn't know anybody in town; Tom was a widower whose entire family had up and moved to Pennsylvania. When I told him that I'd won Powerball, he'd barely blinked an eye. After that first day, I stopped by for coffee and a chat whenever the store was open. I never imagined that it would one day be mine.

I loved everything about it. The wooden beams and creaky floorboards. The way it was eternally cool and dim, on even the sunniest of summer days. And the smells...the pumpkin, cinnamon, allspice, cedar...there was nothing better.

At three thirty, my phone buzzed with a text message from Riley. Just the sight of his name on my screen made me smile. *He's only after your money, dummy,* I scolded myself as I opened the message.

Meet me outside Goldwyn at 4?

Maybe... I texted back, my curiosity bubbling up. **What for?**

Just come. And dress warm!

That message had been followed by a wink emoji. Not only did Riley have a surprise for me, but now he was using wink emojis? Did Maple Sugar Crushes cause hallucinations? That would certainly explain why Donnie once thought he saw a sasquatch crossing the street outside The Shaky Maple. Anyway, *whatever* was going on, the thought of seeing Riley again so soon had sent my heart galloping off into the sunset. There was no way I wasn't going to meet him. I quickly finished up what I'd been doing, then went into the small bathroom at the back of the store. I touched up my makeup and brushed my hair. Were we doing something outside? Was that why I needed to dress warmly? Or was he taking me on a tour of the mortuary? With Riley, you never did know.

At five minutes to four I locked up the store and got into my car. It was a quick walk to the funeral home, but now that it was officially freezing outside, I opted to drive. I pulled into a parking space next to Riley's black Honda Civic, and saw him waiting for me under the green and white-striped awning. He was wearing his coat, and the funeral home lights were all turned off, so it didn't look like he was taking me back inside. Thank goodness.

He'd been staring at his phone when I pulled in, but looked up when I slammed my car door. He met me halfway across the parking lot and immediately handed over his phone.

"What's this?" I asked, laughing as I took it from him.

"This is one of those *eyes on you and not my phone* type of things."

"Oh, is it?" I asked, confused. "Where are we going?" There was no way Riley had coordinated any sort of dinner plans with my family.

"You'll see." He held out his left elbow.

"Um…okay." I linked my arm through his, like we were going to the prom. I let him lead me across the street, and then all the way to the opposite side of the common, where we came to a stop in front of the tire swings. The Autumnboro Inn was close, just on the opposite side of the street, and I could see the television through the first-floor window. Audrey, Burt, and Carla were on the couch. The front door opened and Quinn came outside, lighting up a cigarette.

"He *smokes?*" I said, horrified.

Riley nodded. "Every few hours he comes out here. I smelled it on him at the store earlier, didn't you?"

"I can't smell anything but fall spices when I'm at work. I'm going to go yell at him." I took a step toward the inn, but Riley held me back.

"You can yell at him later," he said. "That's not why I brought you over here. I figured we could put on a performance before it got dark." Letting go of my arm, he walked over to one of the tire swings and climbed inside. Then he grabbed the second one and pushed it in my direction.

"You're serious?"

"I've heard there's something very convincing about seeing two people swinging in tire swings."

"Funny," I said, laughing as I climbed in. I twisted the swing around a few times, tilted my head back, and looked up into the branches of the twisty old oak as the rope unwound. Riley swung closer to me, tapping my foot with his black dress shoe. His pants had ridden up about six inches, which, on anyone else, would not have been a good look at all—but to me, he looked just fine. Dizzy, I gently kicked him back.

"Has he noticed us yet?" he asked, turning his back to the inn and facing me.

"I think so," I said. "He's leaning up against the railing. Oh, but now he's going back inside."

"Give it a minute."

A moment later, the screen door slammed again, and now *everybody* was out on the front porch watching us—including my mother, who must have driven over to the inn for a visit.

"Now we're in business," said Riley. With some difficulty, he climbed back out of his swing and came around behind me, giving me a gentle push.

"This is pretty fun," I said, my feet skimming back and forth over the fallen leaves. "I can see why Catrina was so into it." At the mention of Catrina, he pushed me harder, making me laugh.

After a few more swings, Riley suddenly stopped the tire with both hands and spun me around to face him. My heart didn't seem to care that there was a big rubber tire swing between the two of us; it was hammering away like crazy. I looked nervously up, while he looked awkwardly down. What next? Everybody was lined up against the porch railing, gawking at us. What would make us look like a couple in love? Kissing was the obvious answer. As many times as I'd dreamed about kissing Riley over the summer, the thought of faking it in front of everybody on that porch just wasn't appealing at all.

"Come on, Moneybags," he said. "Time for phase two."

"Phase two?" I climbed out of the swing and followed him over to a small cooler that he'd hidden behind the slide. There was a blanket folded on top of it that Riley spread out on the grass. Then he pulled two mini bottles of champagne out of the cooler.

"Oh, wow!" I said, my jaw dropping. "You came prepared. You want that money even more than I thought." I was only joking, but Riley looked at me with a bit of hurt in his eyes.

"I *really* want those two toolbags to get the message," he said, jerking his head toward the inn.

I sank down onto the blanket, watching Riley as he poured us two glasses.

"A toast." He held his glass into the air. "I don't know half of you half as well as I should like, and I like less than half of you half as well as you deserve."

I laughed and raised my own glass into the air. "If the ocean were whiskey and I were a duck, I would swim to the bottom and drink my way up!" I'd heard that one from Uncle Burt when I was ten, and it stuck. We clinked glasses and I took a sip. Riley drained his glass.

"It's *freezing* out here," I said, feeling the frozen ground right through the blanket. "You realize we look ridiculous?"

"Yes, but do we also look convincing?"

I glanced over at the inn. My mother had taken her phone out and was probably trying to zoom in on us. I hesitated for just a moment, then scooted myself between Riley's bent knees, pressing my back against his chest. *One sip of champagne, Josie? Really?* Hey, *he* was the one who'd asked if we looked convincing enough. He wrapped his arms around me and I downed the rest of my champagne.

"Better?" I asked.

"Better."

"Now what?"

"Now we act like we're having a really serious conversation."

"Right. So, um…how's life in Summerboro?"

"Unseasonably warm," he said, his lips close to my ear. "How's your big dinner coming along?"

"Not bad," I said. "I got a permit from the town, and I found a company that can deliver a tent and everything a few days before Thanksgiving. And according to my dad, I have a whole team of chefs at home just waiting to help with the food prep—even though they've never once offered to help me cook on Thanksgiving."

"I can't believe that kid messed up your newspaper ad so badly." He reached over to the bottle of champagne and refilled both of our glasses.

"It's fine," I sighed. "Believe me, the next person to place an ad with Lee Moriarty will have much better results. I'm actually happy to feed everyone that shows up; the only thing I'm worried about is random strangers finding out about my money and not taking no for an answer. Or finding out where I *live*." I shuddered.

"You know, I never really thought about all the things you have to deal with," said Riley, shifting on the blanket, but keeping his arms around me. "You're always so cheerful, even after everything you've told me."

"I have hundreds of millions in the bank, Riley. Cheerful isn't *that* hard."

He chuckled. "You know what I mean. Your ex…your worries about your family…" He paused to take a sip of champagne. "Let me pretend to be the lottery winner this time."

I slowly scooted out from between his legs and turned to face him, rolling onto my knees. "What?"

"At your dinner," he said. "I could pretend to be the lottery winner. The random strangers can try to take advantage of *me*. They can find out where *I* live."

"That's crazy!" I laughed. "Everybody in this town knows us. They already know it's me, silly."

"I'll tell everyone in Autumnboro the plan ahead of time. They'd go along with it! Everybody in this town loves you."

"Oh, Riley," I said, swallowing around the lump in my throat. What could I even say? His idea was sweet, but it was straight out of *Funny Farm*.

"What?" he asked. "If I were your real boyfriend, that's what I would do."

"If you were my boyfriend in a goofball comedy movie, that's what you would do. But you're my fake boyfriend, in *real* life, and doing something like that wasn't part of our deal."

"This isn't about the deal. It's about wanting to protect a person I care about." He reached over and squeezed both of my hands, then looked into my eyes. "Everybody in this town loves you, Josie. Just think about it."

Everybody? He could probably see my heart beating right through my thick winter coat. The way he was looking at me and holding my hands could all be part of the act for our audience across the street. But the words? Nobody over at the inn could hear the words he'd said. *It's about wanting to protect a person I care about.* As I looked into his dark eyes, all the feelings I'd been fighting since the summer washed over me. Both Amy and my mother's words came back to me. *When the right man comes along, you won't be able to fight it. What are you going to do? Turn and run away?*

I slid my hands up to his wrists and gently pulled him toward me. There was no resistance, no time to rethink my impulsive decision, before his lips were on mine—warm and soft and tasting of champagne. He paused for a moment, pulling away and looking at me as if trying to decide if this was real or still part of the act. It was one hundred percent real for me. For him? I couldn't say. All I knew was that I needed to get this out of my system. I leaned forward into his space, one hand on the back of his neck, and kissed him again. He kissed me back with more intensity this time, as if he'd made the decision in his head. *Real.*

It was even better than I'd imagined all summer. Better than I'd ever been kissed in my whole entire life. Better than Dean, better than quarterback Ryan Lavoie in tenth grade, better than the dreams I've had about Jensen Ackles. This kiss was a long time coming on my end, but I couldn't help feeling that maybe it had been for Riley, too. There was just so much heat coming through him. This much passion couldn't possibly have come out of nowhere. Could it?

I slipped my hand into the front of his coat, pressing it against his chest and sliding it down to fiddle with the buttons of his shirt. We could go back to his apartment. Back to his bedroom with the cozy lamps and the rumpled gray sheets. What harm was there, really? Just one night to get him out of my system. I deserved that much; it had been a long summer of pining away. The sound of the door slamming from across the street snapped me rudely back to reality. I looked over to find that everyone had had enough of our impromptu PDA, and gone back inside the inn. I turned back to Riley, my heart still racing. I found him looking at me like I was a hot drink on a cold night.

There was no way one night would get him out of my system. What was I thinking? I *wasn't* thinking, duh. My hormones had hijacked my brain, and the one simple rule I tried to live by— falling in love again will only end in heartache, so don't do it— had almost been forgotten.

"I should get home," I said, forcing the words out. There would be no cozy apartment in Summerboro. No rumpled gray sheets. With nobody watching, we seriously needed to stop.

"Right," said Riley, blowing out a breath as he ran his hand through his hair. "Okay."

Using all my willpower, I started gathering up our things, practically yanking the blanket out from under him. He stepped onto the grass, adjusting his coat and pants. We finished cleaning up in silence, and then set off, wordlessly, across the common. My whole body was still flushed and warm. How had all of that started, again? That's right. *Let me pretend to be the lottery winner,* he'd said. *It's about me wanting to protect a person I care about.*

Well, I certainly wasn't going to let him do that. Moose would kill me if he ever heard me say this, but winning the lottery was *my* burden to bear. I didn't want my parents and my sister to have to deal with the responsibility, and the same went for Riley. If some nut job showed up at his apartment, it would be *my* fault. No thanks. Riley said he wanted to protect a person he cared about; well, so did I.

"I thought about your idea," I said, gently nudging his elbow as we walked. "About pretending to be the lottery winner? I can't let you do it. It's completely nuts. You know that, right?"

"I know," said Riley. "But I'm willing to go a little nuts if it makes things easier on you."

I fought off the urge to pull him to a stop, drop the cooler and blanket, and kiss him again. Instead, I inhaled the clean, crisp mountain air and looked up into the darkening sky.

"Maybe it's me," I said, "but I think it feels like snow."

"Could be," he said.

CHAPTER 18

It didn't snow.

Autumnboro was still stuck in its gray November blah-ness when I arrived at Pumpkin Everything the next morning. Mom and Dad had come along, too, since they hadn't been up to visit the store since I'd first bought it earlier in the year.

I unlocked the door and flicked on the lights. Pixie—in a pink and black plaid belted coat—darted in ahead of us. "Come on in and I'll show you around again!"

Mom, Dad, and Pixie followed me obediently around the store, while I pointed out all the different sections—kitchen, bath, home décor, coffee, specialty foods—with each of their pumpkin-centric merchandise. Mom actually noticed that I'd rearranged a few of the displays, and was impressed with the pumpkin spice deodorant I'd ordered from a woman in Vermont. Dad had a chuckle over the pumpkin spice-flavored Tums. When I told him that he was welcome to take all of them, free of charge, he muttered a polite *no thank you*.

"And the best for last!" I ran over to the fireplace that I'd had converted to electric earlier in the year. I turned it on, watching the flames materialize out of nowhere. Pixie ran over and curled up on the fluffy sheepskin rug. In front of the fireplace were two big, fluffy Lovesac beanbags. Beside the fireplace was a bookcase, filled with books that anybody in town could borrow. Since the Autumnboro Public Library was about the size of a postage stamp, I figured the town could use some help.

"This top shelf"—I pointed—"is full of my friend Amy's horror novels."

Amy hated the fact that I still kept those books around. I explained to my parents how Amy had made a big effort to write a new series of cozy mysteries—books that were still based on the people in our town, but with everybody portrayed in a more flattering light, and nobody getting eaten by monsters. The new series was a tad dull, if you asked me, which was why I liked to keep her older books available. The funny thing was that they were extremely popular among the very same people who'd been *angry* about them last year. A few of the books even had lengthy waiting lists. Go figure.

"I set this up so anybody can just stop by to relax and read." Mom looked at me skeptically, which made me laugh. "And *talk*," I added. "If they want to." Tom once joked that I'd set the area up as a people trap.

"We're so proud of you, sweetheart," said Dad. "If we lived closer, I'd be in here talking with you all the time."

"Thanks, Dad." I beamed back at him, even though his words were bittersweet. If my mother would stop trying to fix me up, I'd love for them to live closer too.

After finishing up the short tour of my store, I took them next door to The Plaid Apple. I introduced my parents to Jackie and ordered a dozen cinnamon apple muffins to go. Next, we went across the street to The Shaky Maple for coffee, then headed down Main Street to the senior center. I dropped the fresh muffins off in the kitchen, then I introduced my parents to Deb. I showed them the Josie Morgan Fitness Studio, the shuffleboard table, and the place where I stood to call bingo numbers.

"Let's make one more quick stop," I said, as the door to the senior center closed behind us. The office of *The Autumnboro Times* was just a few steps away.

I opened the door to find Lee alone in the office, standing at one end of his desk and bouncing a ping-pong ball into a red plastic cup. The sound of the door made him miss his shot, sending the ping-pong ball ricocheting around the office. Pixie took off after it.

"Beer pong?" I said, picking up the ball. "Seriously?"

"Slow morning," he said, plucking the ball out of my hand and tossing it into his desk drawer, along with the cup. "And it's a Friday. You're not gonna tell my boss, are you?"

I rolled my eyes. "Add it to the list of things I let you get away with."

"Thanks. So, what's up? Who are they?"

"These are my parents. Mom, Dad, this is my friend, Lee Moriarty."

I waited for the murmuring of hellos to be finished, then I placed one hand on my father's shoulder and looked at Lee. "My dad, here, used to be a teacher." Then I placed my other hand on Lee's shoulder and looked at Dad. "Lee, here, is thinking about *becoming* a teacher."

"Is that right?" asked Dad, his interest piqued. "What subjects are you interested in?"

Lee shrugged.

"Grade level?"

Lee shrugged. "I've only been giving it serious thought since last week. After I met your daughter."

Dad's eyes lit up, the way they used to on the first day of a new school year. "If you have a few minutes," he said, "I'd love to discuss it with you. I can answer any questions you have. Maybe figure out your next steps?"

Lee looked around the vacant office, then down at his nearly empty desk. "Sure. Why not?"

"Great!" I reached into my purse and pulled out the brochures I'd picked up from White Mountains Community College. I tossed them onto Lee's desk, then I put my arm around my mother and guided her back toward the door. "You two take your time. Mom and I will finish up the tour and we'll meet you later! Come on, Pix."

I turned to my mother as soon as we were back out on the street. "So, do you want to go see the funeral home?"

She raised her eyebrows. "You know, Josephine, if you ever start giving these tours professionally, I'd advise *skipping* the funeral home."

I snorted. "You're funny. I meant to stop in and say hello to Riley."

I'd tossed and turned all night, replaying what had happened between us on the common, too hot and bothered to sleep. I'd awoken this morning feeling heartsick, lonely, and basically dying to see him. I was hopeless.

"Ah," said Mom. "I should've known. You two certainly seemed to be having a good time last night." She glanced at me as we walked, and my cheeks warmed. I'd never intended to have a full-on make-out session in front of everybody. In hindsight, it was a bit embarrassing.

"Sorry about that," I said. "It's just...you know...*when the right man comes along, you won't be able to fight it.*" She couldn't argue with her own words, could she?

"Well, Dylan and Quinn weren't too thrilled about it," said Mom. "They took off late last night to some bar in North Woodstock. Carla said she didn't hear them come back until two o'clock in the morning. And she thinks they brought home *girls.*"

"Good," I said. "I'm happy for them."

Mission accomplished, thank you Riley. Although, the thought of strange girls hanging around at the inn made me anxious. I needed to go over there to check on everything, never mind bringing in the mail and watering the plants, like I was supposed to be doing. Kit and Amy would probably be calling soon to check in.

The three of us arrived at the funeral home, walked up the brick path beneath the striped awning, and I opened the door. Artie Goldwyn was sitting at Maggie's desk, peering at her computer through his dark-rimmed glasses. I pushed the door shut, unzipped my coat, and shoved Pixie inside.

"What on Earth are you doing?" asked Mom.

"Dogs aren't technically allowed inside," I whispered. But I wasn't about to leave her outside, either. I opened the door again. "Hi, Artie! Mom, this is Artie Goldwyn. He owns the place." Artie looked up, his eyebrows pulling together at the sight of the big bulge in my coat, probably wondering if he should offer me congratulations.

"It's nice to meet you," said Mom. "Your funeral parlor is lovely."

"Thank you," said Artie, looking back at the computer just as Pixie did a complete three-sixty inside my coat. He looked up at us again. "Do either of you know anything about QuickBooks? With Maggie on vacation, I'm in a bit over my head here."

"I use it at the store," I said. "I'm sure I could figure—"

"Move," said Mom, who'd already darted around me and was practically shoving Artie out of his chair. "I managed a small office for thirty years." Her eyes had lit up and she looked almost as excited as Dad when I'd left him with Lee.

"I'm going to go look for Riley," I said, taking a few steps toward the back office. "He's not with a client, is he?"

"No," said Artie, glancing up at me. "He's all yours."

He's all yours. With Artie and my mom here, I wasn't as freaked out as I normally was about wandering around the funeral home. Instead of fear, my stomach filled with butterflies as I walked toward Riley's office. I knocked gently on the open door.

"Hi," I said.

"Oh, hey," he said, looking up from the yellow legal pad he'd been writing on. His eyes widened at the bulge in my coat. "Is there something you need to tell me?"

I laughed as I stepped into his office and closed the door, letting Pixie out of my coat.

"Stay quiet, please."

She ran over and curled up beside Riley's space heater. I took a seat in the chair on the opposite side of his desk, looking over the bookcase behind him. It was mostly filled with legal books and books on advance funeral planning. He also had his framed diploma from UNH, a Halloween skeleton holding a sign that said *Out to Lunch,* several Funko Pop figures—Jay and Silent Bob, The Crow—and a completed Lego Batmobile. On his desk, just behind the keyboard, was the little Pikachu figure I'd given to him as a joke when he moved to Summerboro. Pikachu in sunglasses, sitting on a beach chair, festive pink drink in hand.

"So," I said, my eyes back on Riley's face. He leaned over to switch off his space heater, before remembering that Pixie was enjoying it.

"So," he repeated, sitting back up and tapping his fingers nervously on his phone screen. "What's up?"

"My mom's out there showing Artie how to use QuickBooks," I said, tilting my head toward the front office. "I have no idea what came over her, but she actually looked *excited* about it. My dad's over at the newspaper office talking Lee into becoming a teacher. He looked pretty excited too, and I'm taking full credit for that one. The rest of my family is taking Granny over to Grayson's for lunch. Uncle Burt says he's going to beat the turkey challenge." The Grayson's Turkey Challenge is when one person eats a ten-pound turkey, down to the bones, in thirty minutes or less. If you succeed, the entire table eats for free. If there's anybody who can do it, it's Uncle Burt.

Riley smiled. "You like having them here."

"When my mom's not on my case about dating, and my relatives aren't acting like jerks, then yes." I rolled my eyes. "It's kind of nice having them here."

"How would you feel about getting away from them for a day?" asked Riley. "Like, tomorrow?"

"What's going on tomorrow?"

"There's this Pokémon Go thing at Santa's Village. I thought you might want to come."

"To *Santa's Village*?" I laughed. Santa's Village was a Christmas-themed amusement park up in Jefferson. They had reindeer roller coasters, and elves, and lots of hot chocolate. Most people didn't go there unless they were accompanied by a toddler. I hadn't been since I was a kid.

"You have a problem with Santa's Village?"

"Well, no," I said, thinking it over. It was actually a pretty fun place, especially at this time of year. Cold, but fun. But a whole day alone with Riley? It had taken all my willpower to break away from him last night on the common. Subjecting myself to an entire day of being drawn together by the need for body heat would be tremendously stupid.

"I thought it might be good for you to get out of this town for a while."

"I get out of this town *plenty*."

"You do not," he insisted. "You live in this Autumnboro-sized bubble because you're afraid if you leave your bubble, something might happen to you, and your family will go off the deep end after they inherit your money. You told me this yourself."

"Okay, well, do you really think that taking me to Santa's Village is going to help? It's not exactly the same as flying off to Bora Bora." Ever since Lee had mentioned those ocean huts, I had to admit they'd been on my mind.

"You want to go to Bora Bora?" It sounded like more of an offer than a question. His eyes moved down to my lips and I felt queasy.

"Nope."

"Then come with me." He drummed his fingers on his desk. "It's more than you would normally do this weekend. Maybe it'll inspire you to book a trip to Alaska."

"Pixie *hates* the cold."

"You know you can leave her home, right? There's this thing called a kennel..."

My jaw dropped. "How *dare* you?"

Riley smiled. "Come on. I'll have you back in time to tuck Pixie into bed."

I tried to tell myself that he'd be focused on his phone and his game the entire time; but with the sparks jumping across the desk between us, I knew that wasn't true. He'd been thinking about last night just as much as I had. This whole fake relationship had gotten completely out of hand in a matter of days. Going to Santa's Village would lead to nothing but heartache. I knew better than to say yes. I wasn't an *idiot.*

"Okay," I said. "I'll go."

CHAPTER 19

⚜

"This one…or this one?"

I swapped my white wool beanie with the dusty rose pom-pom for a gray, fur-trimmed bucket hat, before turning around to face Pixie. She barked. She'd also barked when I put on the white one, which wasn't very helpful. Both good, or both terrible?

"Let's play it safe," I said, taking off the bucket hat and replacing it with a slouchy, burgundy newsboy cap. I arranged my hair over my shoulders, before presenting myself to Pixie. She turned around in a circle, lay down on the bed, and closed her eyes. Perfect!

I was a bundle of nerves, waiting for Riley to pick me up for Santa's Village. I tried to play it cool in front of my family (I figured it would seem suspicious if I looked like I was about to throw up, when we'd supposedly been dating for weeks). When Granny took one look at me and asked if I'd eaten something bad for breakfast, I gave up trying to appear calm, retreated to my bedroom, and changed my clothes a million times.

Finally, he was here, standing at the door in jeans and his black North Face coat, saying hello to my family and handing me a hot pumpkin spice latte that he'd picked up on the way. Then we were in his warm car, inches apart, settling in for the hour-long drive to Jefferson, through mostly wooded and sparsely populated roads. I'd never been in his car before, and as we started our journey in silence I took in every last detail. Pack of gum. Sunglasses. Extra napkins in the passenger door. Who'd put those there? I pictured Catrina Corman and felt a huge wallop of jealousy. Briefcase on the backseat. Loose form on the floor titled "Memorial Service Advance Planning Worksheet." Inspection sticker due in July.

I took a sip of my latte and looked over at Riley, soaking up the angles of his face while his eyes were on the road. I watched his fingers on the wheel, the way his thumb tapped along with the radio. I'd tried to put Christmas music on the radio, but he'd said *No Christmas music until after Thanksgiving.* Scrooge.

"Got any more questions for me, Moneybags?" he asked, glancing over.

"Huh?"

"Like we were doing at The Plaid Apple. You ask, I answer."

"Really?" I didn't want to force him into having a conversation. I was certainly enjoying the drive, and the view. Still, since he'd asked...

"Really."

"Okay."

I asked him to tell me more about his gothy high school self, what his college roommates were like, what it had been like coming back to Autumnboro after four years away. Favorite song, favorite color, favorite place to eat at the mall? How did he feel about capuchin monkeys? He told me more about himself on that car ride than he had over the entire summer. Maybe it was the fact he was driving that put him at ease—his eyes focused on the road, rather than me. Whatever it was, I was disappointed when we finally arrived at Santa's Village. I'd have happily continued straight through to Canada.

The parking lot was busy. There was a crowd here for the Pokémon Go event, on top of the regular weekend tourists. Children bundled into winter coats and ski pants, wearing Santa hats and reindeer antlers, were heading for the gates alongside packs of underdressed teenagers staring at their phones. Riley was clearly in his element, and I could feel the joy radiating off of him as soon as we stepped out of the car.

"What are you smiling about?" he asked, narrowing his eyes at me.

"You're *glowing*." I laughed. "Like a pregnant lady."

We paid our admission and entered the park, where "Frosty the Snowman" was blasting over the loudspeakers. All the Christmas lights were on and twinkling, despite it being eleven o'clock in the morning. We crossed a set of railroad tracks and then stopped to get our bearings. There was something called Elf University up ahead on the right, and the Jolly Lolly candy store to the left. A gingerbread man skipped by, goofily trying to catch Riley's attention, but his eyes were already fixed on his phone.

"Where to?" I asked.

"This way." He grabbed me by the hand, and off we went.

The next couple of hours were a blur of racing around the park, laughing as we dodged crowds of teenagers, and searching for PokéStops. Between stops, I convinced Riley to go on a few rides—The Skyway Sleigh, Rudy's Rapid Transit Coaster—and he convinced me to feed a real, live, terrifying reindeer (who nearly bit my fingers off). Eventually, we stopped for food at the Burger Meister food court, where we sat for over an hour, just thawing out and talking, before heading back out.

The sun was starting to get low, and Riley was about to drag me all the way back to the other side of the park, when I held up my hand for him to stop.

"I need a break!" I said. "I'm freezing! I'm buying us hot chocolate." I walked over to the nearest drink stand and ordered two big cups with whipped cream. They'd be ice cold in about three minutes.

"Here," I said, holding out a cup. Riley put his phone into his pocket and took it.

"You're shivering," he said, eying my cup as it wobbled in my hand. "Maybe we should get out of here."

I was shivering, that was true. But I still wasn't ready for our day to end. Right on cue, Santa's Express Train came to a stop a few feet away. The train was tiny, and each of its sleigh-shaped seats had a big red and green blanket draped across.

"Soon," I said, pointing to the train and heading straight for it. "But first, we're going on *that*."

We squeezed into a seat near the back, Riley's knees bumping the seat in front of us.

"Do you know how many sick kids have used this blanket?" he asked, gingerly lifting a corner of it between two fingers. "It probably has frozen boogers all over it."

"Don't care," I said. I shook out the blanket and threw it across the both of us, reveling in its warmth. I snuggled in closer to Riley, hopelessly drawn to his body heat. The little voice in the back of my head—the one that would normally be telling me this was a very bad idea—was nowhere to be found. Frozen to death, most likely. A moment later, Riley's arm was around my shoulders. His other hand was holding the hot chocolate, which meant that his phone was still in his pocket and all of his attention was on me.

"Better?" he asked, giving me a gentle squeeze.

"Better."

Yes, it was warmer, but now I had a whole new set of problems. I was hyper-aware of every tiny movement I made. Legs and knees touching under the blanket. His chin against my hair. If I turned to the right, my lips would be right against his neck. Bare skin. That jawline. *Why are you doing this to yourself?* The little voice was back, apparently warmed up enough to start nagging at me again. *He's taking your money and he's going on vacation. Get a grip.* I sighed into my hot chocolate.

As the train rolled to a stop at Jingle Bell Junction, an elf skipped up to our seat and tried to give Riley a high-five. Riley just shook his head.

"Scrooge," I mumbled.

"Scrooge, huh?" He looked down at me, pretending to be offended.

I nodded. "You wouldn't let me play Christmas music in the car, and then you wouldn't chest bump that snowman by the Ferris wheel."

"Okay, well, how about this for a Scrooge…I don't want your money anymore."

I narrowed my eyes and pulled slightly away, trying to get a better look at his face. "What are you talking about?"

"The money for my trip," he said, as the train started moving again. "I've been giving it a lot of thought, and I realized that I don't want it anymore. I never should have asked you for it in the first place." He took his arm off my shoulders and turned as much as he could in the tiny seat, so we could see each other better.

"Oh," I said, not quite knowing what to make of this news. "It, um, it wasn't really the fact that you'd *asked* for it that upset me, Riley. I would have given it to you in a heartbeat, if you'd just been your normal moody self. But instead, you went and acted like…" I trailed off, shaking my head.

"I know," he said, softly. "And I'm sorry. I didn't know about your history back then. But you have to know by now that it wasn't an act."

My cheeks burned, despite the cold. What was he saying?

"When you stopped coming by my office over the summer," he continued, "I noticed. Like, *really* noticed."

"Really?"

He ran his fingers down the tendrils of hair peeking out from under my hat. "Really."

I was frozen to my seat. Literally, yes. But figuratively, too. My chest was tight, my fingers gripping the underside of the seat. There was a lump in my throat and my mouth had gone dry. Half of me wanted to throw myself into his arms, while the other half realized we were riding a train around a children's amusement park. I slid closer and kissed him on the cheek.

"You had a crush on me?"

"Something like that."

I smiled. "I had a tiny one, too."

"Had?"

Before I could clarify that as of the current moment, my crush was still majorly active, his lips were on mine. *This will not end well*, said the tiny voice in the back of my head. I ignored it for a few more minutes, which wasn't too hard to do. Logical thoughts were in short order at the moment. It wasn't until one of the teenagers in the park wolf-whistled that I snapped back to reality.

"Riley, I can't," I said, pulling away.

"We could go back to the car?"

"No, it's not the train that's the problem." I slid back a few inches across the seat. "It's this—" I motioned back and forth between us. "It's *us*."

"I kind of like us."

"Okay, not *us*," I clarified. "*Me*. I can't have a normal relationship like other people. I've tried before, and it never...it just doesn't work out."

"You tried *once*," he said. "With someone who was a total jerk. I don't care a thing about your money, Josie. This has nothing to do with that."

"But you will care. Someday."

"I won't."

I sighed. We could argue this for eternity, when all I wanted to do was get back to kissing. But we couldn't. As soon as my family went back to Massachusetts, this relationship—whatever it was, real or fake—it had to end. Being dumped by Dean was one thing. Being hurt that way by Riley? I didn't think I'd ever come back from that.

"Look," I said, "I'm going to give you the money for the trip. I *want* to. You looked so happy when we got here. If anybody deserves the chance to play Pokémon Go around the world, it's you."

Riley smiled and shook his head. "You think I looked happy because of the game? I was happy because I'd just spent an hour alone in a car with you, having an actual conversation without second-guessing every word I said." He studied my face. "I'm sorry that it took me all summer and a fake relationship to finally relax around you."

Tears filled my eyes. All last summer, Riley Parker had had a crush on *me*.

"I was sort of hoping," he continued, "that when I finally got to that point, you'd still be waiting."

"You're going on that trip," I said, swiping at my eyes. "End of story."

The train came to a stop at the next station, but we didn't move.

"Come with me, then," said Riley.

"What?"

"If you're insisting that I go on this trip, then come with me. See the world with me. Get some joy out of that money."

"Riley, I *can't*. I have the store, and Pixie, and..." I trailed off. What I had was a hotel room in Australia burned into my memory. Waking up in a foreign country, alone and abandoned. Used. More tears brimmed and spilled down my cheeks.

"Hey," said Riley, reaching for my hand. "Look at me. I think you just need a reset. We go on this trip together, and we come home to Autumnboro together. You and me, start to finish. It's the only way you'll trust me, and maybe not even then. But at least you can say that you gave it a shot, right?"

"I don't know," I said. I'd finally had enough of the Santa Express and wanted to get off, but it had already started moving again. I could probably jump, since we were moving about one mile per hour, but my feet were too frozen to trust. I just stared at the empty French fry box beneath the seat in front of us.

"Well, I do know," said Riley. "I know that you need to talk to your family. Tell them about your fears. Tell them everything that you told me. You can't just make *not dying* your one goal in life."

"I thought not dying was the *ultimate* life goal?"

"I want more than that," he said, ignoring my attempt at humor. "I want more than that with you."

I took a deep breath. I needed this to be clear and firm, even if it broke my heart. This pain was nothing compared to what it would feel like two years from now.

"Well, that's not what *I* want," I said, trying to keep my voice steady. "I had a crush on you, and you had a crush on me, and now we've cleared the air. And, yes, it was *very* nice while it lasted, but it's never going to be anything more than that. I'm trying to protect the both of us."

"Don't I get a say in that?"

Maybe if it had been one thing or the other—a relationship with Riley, or traveling around the world—I'd have been able to take the chance. But risking my heart, on top of putting aside my fears? It was too much.

I still hadn't responded by the time the train pulled into the station closest to the park exit. I picked up my purse and stepped off the train, Riley following behind. His phone was back in his hand, and he tapped away at the screen as we walked through the parking lot. It was a long and silent drive home. Even with a million thoughts and regrets swirling around in my mind, I couldn't think of a single thing to say.

CHAPTER 20

Riley texted me early the next morning.

My stomach twisted itself into knots at the sight of his name on my phone screen. I'd barely slept all night, second-guessing everything I'd said on the Santa Express. At two thirty a.m., I'd almost jumped into my car and driven to Summerboro. But I stayed put. The decision I'd made was as much for Riley as it was for myself. Even if he never ended up hurting me like Dean, he still had no idea what he'd be getting himself into. Nobody did; that's why they kept on buying lottery tickets. It wasn't all shopping sprees and fancy cars. Riley would be committing himself to a lifetime of guilt, of being hounded for money, of having friends and family, and people like Moose, looking at him with bitterness and jealousy.

Riley was thoughtful and perceptive; eventually he'd realize that I was right. I was meant to use my money to do good in the world, but I was meant to do it alone. I was Batman—if Batman owned a country store in northern New Hampshire. I was okay with that.

Only, as I lay in my bed the next morning, I felt heartsick and miserable, and not at *all* like Batman. Even though I wanted Riley to see that I was right, I kept clinging to a pathetic hope that he might continue to press the issue. I took a deep breath and opened the text.

Driving down to PA. Decided not to miss turkey day with the family after all.

Or, he was leaving. My stomach sank. I closed my eyes and pressed the phone against my forehead. This was a *good* thing. I needed the space.

Okay, I texted back. **Drive safe.**

I debated adding a heart emoji or maybe a turkey face, but decided against both. We were unemotionally stating the facts, which was also a *good* thing. Cutesy emojis would only confuse things.

Sorry to cut the fake boyfriend thing short. Hope this doesn't mess up anything with your family.

No worries, I wrote. **I think we convinced them.**

I waited a few more minutes, but there were no more texts coming. He was probably already in his car, Maple Sugar Crush in the console, heading for the highway. I dragged myself out of bed to shower and dress. The house was quiet—Mom, Dad, and Granny were all still asleep—as I went downstairs to the kitchen. I wrangled Pixie into a sweater, let her outside to pee, and made myself a cup of coffee.

Since I was already feeling morose, I figured it was a good time to swing by and check on the inn. Hopefully Riley wouldn't mention anything about *that* to Kit and Amy, when he got down to Pennsylvania. The last thing I needed was them freaking out and flying back up here early.

I loaded Pixie into the car and drove into town. It was early, but The Plaid Apple was busy with breakfast customers. People were milling around on the chilly sidewalk, waiting for tables. Moose was across the street, unlocking the door to the mini mart, big black tumbler in hand. I waved, but he looked away.

I drove around the common, the sight of the funeral home

making me even more depressed—which, I supposed, was normal reaction for most people—and pulled into the driveway of The Autumnboro Inn. I would just get the mail and tidy up downstairs. If anybody was still asleep, I wouldn't even need to wake them.

I nearly hyperventilated as soon as I stepped out of the car. Just walking up the path I spotted cigarette butts all over the grass, and crushed, empty beer cans scattered across the front porch. *Seriously?* I shook my head as I unlocked the front door and pushed it open. Pixie ran in ahead of me, then turned around and ran back out, whimpering.

Holy cow. The smell was overpowering.

It wasn't a *bad* smell, it was just…strong. Like the inside of my store, times a thousand. Scrunching up my nose, I stepped inside, Pixie following cautiously behind. Everything seemed normal over by the reception desk, except for the fact that it was freezing inside. Then I looked into the sitting area.

Take-out food containers, plates, cups, and empty cans were strewn all over the floors and coffee tables. Somebody's khaki pants were tossed over the back of the couch, and a lacy pink bra hung from a lamp. The television was still on and there was a dark purple stain on the carpet, beside a toppled wineglass. One of the windows was wide open.

Also, every single scented candle was lit.

I ran to shut the window as the long, wispy drapes blew dangerously close to a candle on the end table. Then I ran around, blowing out the rest of them, my heart pounding away in my chest. They could have burned down the inn!

I picked up the khaki pants and checked the size. Uncle Burt or Randy would never fit into them. I circled the pink, lacy bra, looking at it from all angles. There no way that thing belonged to Aunt Carla or Audrey. No, this mess had Dylan and Quinn written all over it.

Kit and Amy had asked me to bring in the mail and water the plants, and I'd gone and moved in two reckless dumbbells who almost burned the place down. My money could fix a lot of things, but it couldn't replace a nineteenth-century Victorian home that contained all of their childhood memories. I felt sick.

I ran up the stairs and started pounding on both Dylan and Quinn's doors. No answer. I rushed back downstairs, grabbed the spare keys, and ran back up. I unlocked Quinn's door first and barged right in. He was asleep in bed with a pile of blonde hair snuggled up beside him.

"Rise and shine!" I yelled, shaking the bed. Then I stormed over to Dylan's room and threw open his door. "Check-out time!" I pounded on the blankets. The redhead who was beside Dylan, squinted at me with one eye as I raised all the shades. I walked back out into the hall, waiting until both guys had staggered out in their boxers, looking blurry-eyed and hungover. The two girls stayed in bed, under the covers.

"What time is it?" asked Quinn.

"*Early*," I said. "Party's over! Take your junk, take your girl-friends, and take a hike!"

"What's wrong?" asked Dylan.

"What's wrong?" I narrowed my eyes. "What's *wrong* is that you two left every candle in this place *burning* last night. Next to an open window! And there's lingerie hanging from a lamp!"

"Are you jealous?" asked Dylan, giving me a dopey smile as he took a step toward me, his eyes still half-closed.

"Out!"

"You know, you're the one who told us to go to that bar in North Woodstock," said Quinn. "I don't see how you can be jealous *now*."

I rolled my eyes and took my place at the top of the stairs, arms folded across my chest. "I'll be waiting right here until you're packed."

The door to Uncle Burt and Aunt Carla's room cracked open. "What's going on out there?" asked Burt.

"Nothing," I said. "Go back to sleep." He shrugged and went back into his room.

Dylan and Quinn gave each other *We really dodged a bullet with this one* looks, before going back into their rooms. There were a few moments of silence when I thought maybe they'd decided to ignore me and get back into bed. But then I heard the sound of slamming drawers and rustling sheets, and female voices saying "Who was *that*?" and "What's *her* problem?"

Before long, all four of them were sloppily dressed and filing past me down the stairs. I followed them down, making sure they handed me back their room keys. I couldn't believe I'd actually let them stay here. What had I been *thinking*?

I hadn't been thinking. I'd been resentful that Kit and Amy hadn't asked for my help with the inn. I'd been hurt. I'd felt as if they'd been using me for my money, just like everyone else. So, I'd gone and done this selfish thing, and now look what could have happened. If I weren't worried about further staining the carpet, I could have easily thrown up.

I'd almost pushed the last of them out the front door, when Quinn suddenly doubled back.

"Forgot my pants," he mumbled, darting into the sitting area. He was stumbling and walking erratically—probably still drunk from last night—when his foot caught a power cord running across the floor. It was the cord connected to the lights around Tom's model stagecoach.

What happened next was a bit of a blur. I let out a strangled yelp as Quinn went tumbling to the ground. The small stand that the model stagecoach was sitting upon toppled forward in horrible, car crash-like slow motion. The glass case hit the wood floor first, with a terrific shatter. Then Tom's model stagecoach—the delicate one that he'd spent seven years of his life painstakingly building—crashed to the floor.

Quinn and I blinked at each other as the other three hurried out the front door.

"Get out," I hissed.

He got to his feet, grabbed his pants, and bolted.

* * *

I SANK TO THE FLOOR, remaining motionless for several minutes. Pixie put her head down in my lap. I'd narrowly escaped burning down the inn, only to cause the next worst thing I could possibly imagine. Poor Tom. He was going to be devastated! He was going to *hate* me. I put my face in my hands and groaned.

Finally, I stood and put Pixie in the car so she wouldn't cut her paws, then I went into the kitchen to find a dustpan and some towels. I spent the next half hour carefully cleaning up all of the broken glass—thankfully none of it had gotten into the carpet—wrapped it all up, and placed it into a cardboard box.

Then, I put all the broken pieces of Tom's model stagecoach into another cardboard box, with a soft towel lining the bottom, like an injured baby bird. I still had a sliver of hope that maybe I could glue it back together. I'd inspect it more closely once I was back at the store. I cleaned up the rest of the sitting room, the front porch, and the lawn, and I threw away the pink, lacy bra (I doubted its owner would be back for it). When I was finished, I brought both cardboard boxes out to my car, and drove to Pumpkin Everything.

I had only just started googling *model stagecoach repair* and watching instructional videos on YouTube, when a tour bus, on its way to Maine, stopped off at The Plaid Apple for lunch. Tourists started trickling into my store soon after, to kill time before their bus left. I couldn't let them find me staring at my computer as if I'd committed some horrific crime that I was trying to figure out how to cover up. Not that googling *model stagecoach repair* was the same as googling *how to dispose of body*, but I felt just as guilty.

Even if I could actually glue the thing back together, they'd still be able to tell. And once I told them the truth, they'd never trust me enough to let me actually work at the inn. Which was exactly what I deserved.

I tried to shake away my negative thoughts and focus, for the time being, on the customers. Chatting with customers always cheered me up, and even on a day like today, it seemed to do the trick. The bus tour had started in Boston, and was slowly making its way through western Massachusetts, Vermont, and New Hampshire, before heading to Bar Harbor and Acadia National Park in Maine. Most of the people on the tour had flown in from other parts of the country—some from other parts of the world—to enjoy two leisurely weeks on the road.

"We just met!" said one lady, throwing her arm around the shoulders of another. "I'm from Florida, and she's from New Mexico. We were both traveling alone, so we paired up!"

"Lucky us," said the other woman, laughing as she plunked a bobbling turkey headband onto her new friend's head.

They made me smile, all bright-eyed and merry, with so much to look forward to. There were so many possibilities out there…so many people to meet…so many incredible things to see. I had all the money in the world, but those two ladies seemed like the lucky ones.

When the last of the tourists had gone—I'd sent each of them off with a free stick candy of their choice—I settled down again in front of my laptop to wallow. Maybe I should just call Tom right now and explain what happened? Then again, why should I ruin his Thanksgiving? I'd be able to explain and beg for forgiveness much better in person, after they were home.

My cell phone rang and my heart stopped, hoping that it was Riley. It was Amy. Shoot. I hadn't spoken to her since she'd left—I couldn't let it go to voicemail.

"Hi!" I said, trying to sound cheerful and totally normal. "How's it going? How's Pennsylvania?"

"It's great!" said Amy. "I met Catherine Zeta-Jones!"

"No way!"

"Yep. Mom took us on a QVC studio tour. Grandpa got to shake hands with that guy that sells the smoked brisket."

"Aw, tell Tom I'm *so* jealous," I said. "It's, like, my dream to meet the smoked brisket guy."

"Really? I think he might be single. If you come down here sometime, my mom will introduce you to anybody you want. You're her number-one customer."

"I will definitely do that," I said. "Someday. Totally."

"So, how's the inn? Nothing to report?"

"Nothing to report!" I practically yelled. "Plants watered. Mail collected!"

"Good, good," she said. "So, Riley's on his way down here, but you probably knew that already."

"I heard," I said, trying to keep my voice as uninterested as possible.

"To be honest, I was sort of hoping something might have happened between you two since we left. But I guess not."

"Nope. I've barely even seen him."

"Too bad," she said, a hint of exasperation in her tone. "Riley's a good apple."

A lump formed in my throat. He *was* a good apple. Maybe the *best* apple out there, and I'd left him on the ground to rot with the rest of them.

"He's a good apple," I said. "I'll give you that. But, you know, you don't just throw all the good apples to the wolves, Amy. That's like, a serious waste of apples. You have to *protect* them. Turn them into pies. Or those dolls that look like old people."

"*What?*"

"Never mind. Look, I have to go. Have a great Thanksgiving!

Send my love to everybody." *Except for Riley.* "Tell them I miss them!"

"Okay," said Amy. "We all miss you too. See you soon!"

"See you soon," I said weakly, my eyes drifting to the box of smashed up stagecoach parts on the floor beside me. Way too soon.

What a mess.

CHAPTER 21

"I received a text message from Quinn today," said Mom, as soon as I'd returned home from work that evening. She was sitting at the kitchen table, eating coffee cake with Granny. "He said you threw him and Dylan out? Literally threw them out the front door?"

"I wish it had gone that smoothly," I said, plopping down in the chair across from her and rubbing my face. "Did he tell you *why* I threw them out?"

"He said you came in like a crazed—I refuse to say which noun he used—and barely even gave them time to pack."

I rolled my eyes. "Did he mention that they practically trashed the inn, left about a thousand burning candles unattended *all night*, and left women's underwear hanging from a lamp?" I counted off each item on my fingers. "Oh, and Quinn tripped and smashed Tom's handcrafted model stagecoach."

"Smashed *what?*" asked Lee, walking into the kitchen followed by my father.

"Tom's model stagecoach," I said, slowly. "I have it in a box at the store, smashed to bits. What are *you* doing here?"

Lee was holding a notebook in one hand. Dad was looking

scholarly, dressed in an argyle sweater vest that he had, for some reason, brought along with him to Autumnboro.

"We've been looking at schools online," said Lee. "Did you know it's only a twenty-five-minute drive to Plymouth State? That's far enough that my mom won't pop in, but not far enough to make laundry inconvenient." He turned and gave my dad a high-five.

"I'm going to help with his application and essay," said Dad. "We're going to keep in touch!"

"That's so great," I said, smiling at both of them. At least *something* had worked out right this week.

"Want to stick around and watch the game?" asked Dad, pointing toward the living room.

"Seriously?" asked Lee, his eyes widening. "In there? On the big screen? What is that thing, eighty-two inches?"

"One-oh-five," I muttered. Without another word, Lee took off into the living room.

"WHAT WAS that about women's underwear hanging from a lamp?" asked Granny, as soon as we were alone.

"It was pink and lacy," I said. "And just *dangling* there."

"And it was *theirs*?" Granny whispered.

"No, no, no." I chuckled. "It belonged to one of the girls they brought home from the bar last night. Can you believe the type of men she tries to set me up with?" I jerked my thumb toward my mother, then turned to look at her. "I can't believe you brought those two up here after I told you *so* many times to please stop trying to fix me up. And then you gave me that whole story about how their families abandoned them for the holiday because you *knew* I was too nice to send them home."

"I know," said Mom, putting her face into her hands, her shoulders slumping forward. "I'm sorry. They were just so eligible! They were good looking, they were your age, and we were already on a first-name basis! I honestly thought I was doing you a favor."

"I know you did," I sighed. "But even if you couldn't understand why I didn't want you to fix me up, I wish you would have at least *listened* to me. You need to trust that I know what I'm doing."

"You're right," she said, nodding. "I let my friends get under my skin. All they talk about is which of their children is getting married at which extravagant venue. They've got nothing better to do! It's actually been quite nice getting back into the *real* world for a while. Anyway, I see now that you were perfectly capable of finding somebody without my help; even if he is a little…morbid. We're all so happy for you, Josephine. Really."

"*Riley*," said Granny, her eyes lighting up. "I liked him. When will we get to see him again?"

My heart sank at the look of joy on their faces. When I'd concocted this whole fake boyfriend idea, it had been in the midst of an emergency. I hadn't had any time to really think about what it entailed. I'd never considered the fact that my family might actually be happy I'd finally found someone after Dean. I'd never considered the fact that later on, they might be upset to hear we'd broken up.

"He's, um, he's actually gone down to Pennsylvania to be with his family for Thanksgiving," I said, with a no-big-deal sort of a shrug. "He'll be back, though."

"Good," said Granny, squeezing my hand.

"Wonderful," said Mom.

Lee and Dad cheered from the other room.

* * *

OVER THE NEXT FEW DAYS, I tried to focus all my attention on getting ready for Thanksgiving. The tent, tables, chairs, heaters, and portable toilets were all delivered to the common on

Monday afternoon. There was a bit of snow in the forecast for Wednesday, but it didn't look like more than a dusting. Since Riley had left, I'd been wallowing in Autumnboro's gray November dullness, and was sort of hoping the weather would stay that way for at least a few more weeks. On Monday, my sister Meg finally arrived with her husband Dave, and my two nieces, Nina and Ayla. We had dinner at my house that night—all twelve of us—making it almost feel like an early Thanksgiving.

The difference was that after my talk with Mom, there was no more harping on my love life. My aunt, uncle, and cousins discussed their past few days of exploring Autumnboro (Uncle Burt was one drumstick away from completing Grayson's Turkey Challenge), and Summerboro (Randy wanted to come back next summer for Jet Skiing). Aunt Carla and Audrey had gone for pumpkin facials at Autumnboro's new day spa, and were practically glowing. Audrey even invited me along for next time—"her treat"—which made me laugh. Nobody mentioned my money a single time, which was most definitely some sort of record.

On Tuesday, I put everybody to work setting up tables and chairs on the common, and on Wednesday, we started preparing the food. Once I'd realized that I was going to need more turkeys than I could possibly cook on my own, I'd given Roy a call at the turkey farm. Before I could offer to buy thirty more pies, he'd agreed to provide me with ten pre-cooked, pre-sliced turkeys by Wednesday evening. All I would need to do was reheat them on Thanksgiving Day. He declined any sort of payment—even in the form of pies—and insisted that he was just happy to help.

All of the side dishes still needed to be prepared, so I set everybody to work making mashed potatoes, stuffing, green bean casserole, and candied yams. By the end of it, my kitchen was one big hot mess—Pixie scurried happily around, lapping up anything and everything that fell to the floor—but it had been *fun.* For the first time in a long time, it wasn't just me in the kitchen, preparing Thanksgiving dinner all by myself. With a football game on in the background, we joked and we teased, and we drank cups of homemade caramel apple sangria. Somehow, my most self-centered relatives—who had never been satisfied, no matter how much money I gave them— seemed to have been swept up in the giving spirit of the season. Maybe it was the sangria, but everybody finally seemed *happy*.

I was happy, too. Mostly.

When thoughts of Riley crept in—which was every five seconds, it seemed—I reached for the sangria. But it wasn't helping much, and I was starting to get clumsy. After I'd dropped a spoonful of mashed potatoes directly onto Pixie's head, I put my glass into the sink.

"I'm cut off!" I announced. I paused at the sink, staring out into the darkness. What I wanted, more than anything, was for Riley to come up beside me, his arm around my waist. We would clean up the kitchen, then we'd snuggle on the couch. My reflection stared back at me, frowning and alone.

Shortly after cutting myself off, Burt, Carla, Audrey and Randy retired outside to the hot tub, and Dave took the girls to The Shaky Maple for hot chocolate, leaving me alone with Mom, Dad, and Meg. Granny was dozing in the living room.

"Can we talk for a minute?" I asked, wiping down the kitchen island. The three of them were sitting around the kitchen table, polishing off an apple pie.

"Pull up a chair, sweetheart," said Dad. "What's on your mind?"

"I wish I could have met this Riley," said Meg, as I pulled out a chair. "It's too bad he had to leave right before we got here. But I suppose I'll have more chances."

"That's sort of what I wanted to talk to you about," I said. "Riley. He's, um, he's asked me to go on this pretty big trip with him. To Japan, Europe…all over." I left out the part where we'd be searching for Pokémon. Unimportant, super lame detail.

"That's wonderful," said Dad. "It's been so long since you've done any traveling."

"Do you think he's going to propose?" asked Mom, her eyes widening. She turned to Meg, both of them squeezing hands.

"I'm not going," I said. They dropped hands, their faces falling right along with them.

"Why on Earth not?" asked Meg.

I told them everything I'd told Riley; the lingering effects of the sangria helped me to finally let it all out. I told them how the thought of traveling filled me with anxiety and painful memories. I told them how I worried that if anything ever happened to me, they'd be left to deal with my money and all of the headaches that came with it. I felt ridiculous as I heard the words coming out of my mouth, as if I were completely out of touch with reality. *I want to protect you from the horror of becoming financially secure multi-millionaires.* Just the same, it was how I felt, even if nobody else could understand it. Even if I knew that my reasoning had most likely been warped by heartbreak.

"Oh, Josie," said Meg, staring at me with her chin in her hand. "I just assumed you were leaving everything to Pixie."

"You can't live your life worrying about *us*," said Dad. "I don't ever want to think about something bad happening to you. But if it did, sweetheart, we'd be just fine."

"Dad's right," said Meg. "I mean, we'd mourn your death for a full twenty-four hours, but then we'd be *totally* okay with our inheritance."

"Very funny," I said. "But you're not getting my point. You don't know what it's like having friends and relatives look at you like you're suddenly a different person. Or being hated by people who don't know anything about you, just because you happened to buy a lottery ticket at the exact right time. Never mind the temptation of having this much money at your fingertips. It can be completely overwhelming. I mean, you *saw* what it did to Dean."

"Dean was an ass," said Uncle Burt, stepping through the sliding doors from the back porch. He was wearing a large yellow towel around his waist, and went straight for the refrigerator. "The money had nothing to do with it."

"Of course, the money had something to do with it," I said. "It was too tempting. He cracked."

"Nah," said Uncle Burt, turning to look at me. "Dean was no good from the beginning. If it wasn't the money, it would've been something else. Younger woman. Ponzi scheme. Hang on." He walked back outside and returned a minute later with Aunt Carla. "Tell Josie what we thought of Dean."

"Total ass. From the moment we met him."

"And you never thought to tell me this?" I asked. "You might've saved me a lot of heartache! Never mind half a million dollars!"

"Like you would have listened to *us*," snorted Uncle Burt. "No, you were all googly-eyed in love with that guy. You needed to figure it out for yourself."

There were a few seconds of awkward silence.

"Please don't tell me that you're only figuring it out *now*," whispered Carla.

I put my face in my hands.

"Look," said Uncle Burt, walking over to the table and leaning down across from me, forcing me to look up. "That guy would've ended up hurting you no matter how much money you had in the bank. But he's not the only guy in the world. Get yourself back out there and find someone worthy of blowing all that beautiful money on—well, not *all* that money. Save some for your uncle in his old age, eh?" He straightened up and popped open his beer. "What about that Miley kid? I liked him. Where'd he go, anyway? Don't you dare tell me Thailand."

"It's *Riley*," I muttered. "And he's in Pennsylvania."

"Pennsylvania? What's he doing down there?"

"It's a long story."

"Whatever you say," said Uncle Burt. He walked into the living room and flopped down on the couch, still wrapped in his wet towel.

"Look, honey," said Mom. "If anyone's at risk for getting carried away by money, it's *me*. I know that. But I've got your father here to rein me in. And if you think people aren't already pounding down our door asking for money, you're *wrong*. We deal with it, too, all the time. We don't tell you because we don't want you to worry about us. But trust me, they don't come knocking a second time."

"Your mother has quite a mouth on her," said Dad proudly. "She could give you some tips."

"Really?" I laughed. "I don't believe it."

"Well, you should believe it," said Meg. "Have some faith in us! We've been watching you for years and learning from the best. You've done some great things with that money, Josie, but what you need to do now is get out of your own head. Go do something great for yourself, for once. Whether that means taking that trip with Riley, or taking a spaceship to Mars—"

"Spaceship to Mars?" shouted Uncle Burt, from the living room. "Did she finally book it?"

Meg rolled her eyes. "Whatever it is…just *go*."

CHAPTER 22

I lay awake for hours that night, thinking over everything my family had said. How they'd be okay, no matter what. How I needed to do something great for myself, for once. I'd been convincing myself for so long that their lives would be ruined if anything ever happened to me. I never expected that hearing them say *have faith in us* would mean as much to me as it did. Then there was my aunt and uncle's revelation that perhaps Dean hadn't been the best representation of all the men in the world. I tossed and I turned. Despite everything I thought I knew about dating in my financial situation, maybe I'd been wrong. Sure, there were more Deans out there in the world to be wary of...but there were also Rileys. Actually, there was only one Riley. And I missed him.

When I woke the next morning, I felt unrested and my heart was heavy. But it was Thanksgiving Day, and I had a lot to do. I rolled out of bed and walked into the bathroom. Pixie followed me to the window. I raised the shade and looked outside, temporarily blinded by the whiteness.

Snow!

I gasped and lifted Pixie up so she could see. For the moment,

I was too swept away by the beauty of it to think of anything else. The woods and the river were covered with a gorgeous blanket of soft, white, untouched fluff, and it was still coming down hard.

Five minutes later, I was downstairs, staring out the back windows, slightly less smitten.

"This is *bad*," I said. Everybody was gathered in the living room, watching the Weather Channel. The snow had been coming down hard all night, and wasn't expected to stop until later this morning. According to the weathermen—who I wasn't sure we should be trusting at all, since yesterday they'd predicted nothing but a *dusting*—we'd already had nearly a foot.

"This is really bad," I repeated, turning to look at my family. "That tent wasn't made to hold a foot of snow!"

"Sweetheart, I don't think you're going to *need* that tent," said Dad, motioning to the television. He'd changed it to a local station, where the reporter was advising people to stay inside if they could, as most of the roads were still impassable. I sank down onto the couch. Pixie jumped up beside me and rested her chin on my lap. She was wrapped in her fluffy pink bathrobe, and seemed perfectly fine with the idea of staying in today.

"But it was barely supposed to snow," was all I could mutter, staring at the television. Footage of stuck cars and fallen wires flashed on the screen. A map of the state of New Hampshire showed predicted totals for the White Mountains to be twelve to eighteen inches. I closed my eyes and rubbed the bridge of my nose. "How do they always get it so *wrong?*"

"This could be a good thing," said Dad. "I mean, the people you were worried about showing up and finding out about your money...that's not really a concern anymore, is it? And, you know, *we're* all here." I opened my eyes to find him smiling at me. He didn't mention that Uncle Burt and his family were stranded over at the inn, which I'm pretty sure was on purpose.

I *was* somewhat relieved that tons of potential gold-diggers wouldn't be pouring into town after all. But those people weren't the reason I'd planned this dinner in the first place.

"What about everybody else, though?" I said. "The whole point of this dinner was to help the people in Autumnboro who were going to be alone today. Now, they're *still* going to be alone, while I'm snowed in with my family and tons of food." I put my face in my hands and shook my head. This had not turned out the way I'd planned.

"They might still come," said Granny. "People will do *anything* for free stuff."

I looked up. "You think so?"

Granny nodded. "Gladys Porter once drove fifteen miles through a blizzard for a free hot dog. That was in 1974."

"She did *not,*" said Mom, rolling her eyes.

"We could still set up in the church basement," I said, ignoring my mother as my spirits lifted. "Just in case anybody shows up. I mean, if Gladys Porter drove through a blizzard for a hot dog, people would definitely trudge through a foot of snow for a turkey dinner, don't you think? We'd just have to somehow get all the food and equipment over there."

"Have you heard any plows go by?" asked Mom skeptically.

My house was off the beaten path, and one of the last streets to get plowed, ever. The guy I normally paid to plow my driveway was in Florida visiting his parents for Thanksgiving.

"No," I said. "But, that's okay. I'll figure something out! Just give me some time…and some coffee."

I was in the kitchen pouring myself a cup, when the doorbell rang. My heart froze. Last Thanksgiving, the doorbell had brought Dylan, Quinn, and Brady. This year…*Riley?* My stomach twisted into knots at the idea that it was him. Had he turned around and driven back to New Hampshire? Driven all night through a blizzard to get to me? Gladys Porter had done it for a hot dog, so it wasn't completely out of the question, was it? *Riley.* I'd been thinking about texting him as soon as I'd gotten out of bed this morning, but then the snow situation happened and the moment had passed. But if he was out there right now, I'd throw my arms around him and—

I looked through the peephole to find Moose Moriarty, covered in snow.

"*Moose?*" I said aloud, as all romantic notions vanished in a poof of black smoke. My heart sank.

"Moose?" I said again, pulling open the door. "What the heck are you doing here? Come on in." His heavy brown coat was covered in snow, as were his hair and his bushy beard. In his hands, he held a cardboard box. He stepped into the front hall, stomping his big boots on the mat. I looked past him to the Dodge Ram parked in my driveway. There was a snowplow attached to the front. Without a word, Moose handed me the box.

"What the—"

I took it from him and looked inside, my jaw dropping at the sight of Tom's model stagecoach, no longer in bits. I looked up at Moose, at a loss for words, before carefully carrying the box into the kitchen and placing it gingerly on the counter. "How did you—"

"Lee," he said. "He told me what happened. Then he swiped that box from your store and gave it to me."

I laughed. I knew exactly what he was talking about. Lee had come into Pumpkin Everything the other day, asking if I had any more sticks of women's pumpkin spice deodorant, which was odd enough in itself. When I told him we were sold out, he insisted that I check in the back room. When I returned, he was gone. The little thief.

"And you...you fixed it?" I asked, peering into the box again, afraid to even touch it. But from what I could see, you'd never even know it had been broken.

Moose nodded. "I've done some woodworking. It's a hobby. I used to help Lee with all of his Boy Scout projects. He's always been like a son to me."

"Thank you so much," I said, looking up at him with tears in my eyes. I wanted to wrap my arms around him and give him a big hug, but then something occurred to me. "But why would you help me like this? You don't even *like* me."

Moose rubbed one hand through his wet, bushy beard. "Lee told me how you've been helping him—you and your dad—to look at colleges. I don't know how you convinced him so quickly. I was never able to." He shrugged. "I just wanted to thank you for that. And, you know, apologize, if I was ever"—he cleared his throat and looked up at the ceiling—"rude to you. Or judgmental."

"Aw, Mooose," I crooned, my heart melting. I was about to wrap my arms around his big moosey belly and give him a squeeze, when he held up one hand to stop me.

"Don't go getting all mushy on me, now. I'm still not going to offer you a *job* or anything."

"I wasn't expecting a job offer, silly. At least not today. Can you stay for a while? Have some coffee? Do you like Jingle Bell Spice?" Without waiting for an answer, I poured some into a mug and pushed it into his hands.

"This is what you do with your money?" he asked, looking at the photo of Pixie I'd had custom printed on the side of the mug. It was from the photo shoot we'd done at the pumpkin patch last year.

"You know what?" I said, suddenly tired of feeling guilty about my money. "I could buy a *million* of those mugs and I'd *still* be loaded. What do you think of *that*?" I stared at him until the corner of his mouth twitched into a smile, which turned into a chuckle.

"I think you're nuts," he said, taking a sip of coffee. "But I also think you're a very generous person, so—" He held his mug in the air and clinked it against mine. "You're entitled to do whatever you want."

"Thank you," I said, leaning my elbows on the island. "So, I didn't know you had a plow. I'd have hired you to do my driveway a long time ago."

"Just got one last winter," he said. "After I leave here, I'll be digging out some of the older folks around town. Checking in on them. This storm came out of nowhere."

"Tell me about it," I said, my spirits lifting as an idea came to me. "Before you dig everybody out, though, do you think you could do me one more tiny favor?"

* * *

THE DRIVE into town was a slow one, but with Moose clearing the way it wasn't impossible. My Tesla wasn't cut out for the trek, but thankfully Mom and Dad, and Meg and Dave, both had driven up to New Hampshire in SUVs. We filled the back of both vehicles with containers of food, drinks, buffet servers, warming trays, a small electric fireplace, and decorations. There wasn't enough room left for all the pies, so they rode in the passenger seat of the plow truck, strapped in safely next to Moose. Dave, my nieces, and Granny would join us later, once the roads were safer.

Dad and I looked around in silent awe as we wound our way through the wooded back roads. Clumps of snow occasionally fell from powerlines and tree branches, landing in fluffy white bursts on the windshield. The flakes that were still coming down were much bigger now, landing with satisfying plops on the glass. The storm was slowing down.

As I followed in Moose's tracks, my mind drifted to what Riley might be doing this morning. Was he still in bed, or had he woken up early? Had he found any good Pokémon down in Pennsylvania? My heart ached. I wanted to text him again, but now I was driving, so…later. Not that I even knew what I would say.

The first thing I noticed when we pulled up to the common was that the event tent had completely collapsed. The portable toilets were half-buried. The *Welcome* sign that I'd had custom-made, and staked into the ground, was completely buried. We'd see it again in the spring. We continued around the common to the church, where Moose cleared the way into the parking lot and handed over the boxes of pies. Then, with a toot and a wave, he pulled out and headed for the inn to dig out the rest of my family.

We went inside and turned on the heat. Eight long tables were set up in the center of the room. I covered them in tablecloths and set out the place settings. In the center of each table I placed a flameless pillar candle, surrounded by a wreath of fall flowers. I taped cardboard Thanksgiving decorations to the walls, and plugged in the electric fireplace. I wanted this to feel like *home.* We warmed up the food and set up the serving trays on a long table at the front of the room. On a smaller table, I laid out all the pies—apple, blueberry, pumpkin, pecan—and several boxes of maple sugar candy that I'd taken from my store. Uncle Burt, Aunt Carla, Audrey and Randy arrived at twelve thirty, and by one o'clock, we were ready. The roads had been plowed, and we'd seen a few cars passing by. All of us stood at the ready, aprons on. Serving spoons in hand.

Nothing happened.

Five minutes passed. Then ten.

"Can we eat now?" asked Audrey, after fifteen minutes had gone by.

"They'll *come,*" I insisted. "Gladys Porter did it in 1974 and she didn't even have four-wheel drive."

Finally, at 1:16 p.m., the door creaked open and a gray-haired head poked in. "Hello?"

"Hello!" said Dad. "Come on in!"

An elderly man, a bit stooped over, shuffled slowly inside and looked around.

"Harold!" I called out, recognizing him from the senior center. Harold had lost his wife last year, and didn't have any family nearby. "I'm so glad you made it!" I rushed over to help him with his coat and show him to a seat.

"Josie, darling!" he said. "I should have known you'd be behind this." He smiled and patted me on the cheek.

As I went off to pour him a cup of something warm to drink, the door opened again and several more people filed in, and then even more after that. Some of them I recognized, but there were many I didn't. My heart was full as we loaded up each plate and chatted with our guests. Some were extremely talkative—dying to tell us every last detail about their lives and what had brought them here—while others kept to themselves, simply thanking us for the meal before finding themselves a seat. We had guests of all ages. Most of them were alone—like the man whose flight home to Nova Scotia had been canceled—but there were some couples, as well. One young couple told us that their stove had broken this morning, and if it weren't for us, they'd have been eating Chee-rios for Thanksgiving.

When everybody was seated, I raised my glass for a toast.

"I just wanted to thank all of you for coming out in the snow today," I said, smiling around the room. "I hope you enjoy the food and make some new friends. And may we all be back here again next year."

"Unless you get a better offer," added Uncle Burt.

"Unless you get a better offer," I conceded. "Cheers!"

"Cheers!"

* * *

I WAS EXHAUSTED by the time the last of our guests had gone home, but there was still one more big thing that I needed to do. I'd asked Burt, Carla, Audrey and Randy to pack up their things and sleep over at my house tonight. Kit and Amy would be back in Autumnboro tomorrow, and I needed to make sure the inn was sparkling clean and completely back to normal. It was after ten o'clock when I put Tom's stagecoach back on its display stand, still not believing how good of a job Moose had done. I hadn't been able to replace the glass case yet, so I was planning to tell Kit and Amy that I'd accidentally bumped into it while dusting. Clumsy me.

It was midnight before I fell into my bed back at home. The sound of Uncle Burt snoring from down the hall was oddly comforting. I loved my family, and I was thankful for all of them. Even so, I grabbed a pair of earplugs from my nightstand and put them in. I needed a good night's sleep since I was opening early tomorrow for Black Friday. Main Street had finally been transformed into all of its magical, snowy New England glory, and I was expecting plenty of shoppers.

Also, Riley was coming home.

CHAPTER 23

"Come again!" I said, waving to the woman who'd actually bought out the last of the pumpkin spice Tums. God bless her.

My Black Friday sale had been a huge success. Since Pumpkin Everything didn't typically have sales, customers were excited to stock up on discounted fall items for next year. By four o'clock I was exhausted and ready to close up shop for the day; I hadn't slept well for the second night in a row. I was about to head over and flip the sign on the door to *Closed*, when Amy, Kit, and Tom walked past the front window and threw open the door. I paused for a moment, in the middle of the store, waiting for Riley to come along behind them. It would be so typically him to be lagging behind, staring at his phone. But the door slammed shut without him.

"We're back!" said Amy.

"You're back!" I said, pasting on a smile and giving each of them a hug. "I missed you all so much!"

"We missed you too, darling," said Tom, hugging me back. "But what the heck is *that*?"

I stepped back and followed his gaze to the life-sized Santa

Claus standing beside a tree-shaped rack of Christmas ornaments.

"That," I said slowly, "is a man who dressed up as Santa Claus for Halloween."

"Lovely," said Tom, shaking his head as he went to sit by the fireplace.

"So, did you just get in?" I asked, turning back to Kit and Amy.

"Yep," said Amy. "We came here straight from the airport. We thought we'd stop in and say hello before heading home. Grab the key to the inn. This one's been worrying about it all week, as if we left a child home alone."

"Right," I said, laughing along with her, even though my stomach was roiling with guilt and nerves. "Let me get you that key."

I walked slowly over to the counter and fished the key out of my purse. Instead of turning around again, I paused and stared at the key in my hand. Kit and Amy were my friends and they'd trusted me. I couldn't do this.

"I let my obnoxious relatives and two guys I barely know stay at the inn while you were away!" I blurted out.

"Um, *what?*" asked Kit.

I turned slowly around. All three of them were staring at me, wide-eyed. I swallowed.

"I didn't want them at my house, so I put them up at the inn. But they left candles burning all night long, and they made a huge mess, and they left *underwear* hanging from a lamp." I made underwear hanging from a lamp motions with my hands. "And then, they broke Tom's model stagecoach. But it's fixed now!" I looked pleadingly over at Tom. *"Moose* fixed it! He's like, this amazing woodworker, so...it's not as bad as it sounds."

I walked up to Kit, handed him the key, and burst into tears.

"Oh, boy," said Kit, shrinking back.

Amy put her arm around me and led me over to the chair

171

beside Tom. "Josie, slow down. What the heck are you talking about?"

"I'm *so* sorry," I said, between sobs. "I know that it was a stupid and selfish thing to do, but I was just…I was hurt, okay? Nobody asked for my opinion on a single thing about the inn, and I thought…I thought you guys had used me for my money, just like everybody else." I looked up to see Amy and Kit exchanging glances, as she rubbed circles on my back. "But I had no right to do that, no matter how I felt."

"Josie, we—"

"I cleaned the inn from top to bottom last night," I said, cutting her off. "You'd never even know anybody had been there. But I couldn't just lie to you all forever. I *couldn't*." A fresh wave of tears hit me and I put my face in my hands. "I love you all too much."

"Honey, it's *okay*," said Amy. "Yes, you should have asked us first, but we forgive you."

"Maybe we should go check the place out first?" mumbled Kit.

"Don't listen to him," said Amy. "Josie, look, we were talking while we were away. This trip down to my parents was the first real chance we've had to relax in quite some time, and after a few margaritas, we got to talking about *you.*"

"Me?" I asked, peeking up at her.

"Yes, *you.* Look, we realized we'd been so wrapped up in each other that we hadn't been including you as much as we should have. Yes, you're a silent partner, but you're our *friend* first. We would never take your money and push you away! We're so sorry if we made you feel that way. We love you, too. You know that, right?"

I nodded as a huge weight lifted from my chest. I looked over at Tom. "I really am sorry about your stagecoach. You worked so hard on that."

"It was an accident, darling" he said, batting his hand at me. "To be honest, I'm surprised its lasted as long as it has. Every so often, Lillian would threaten to throw it away, along with the rest of my junk." He smiled fondly at the memory of his late wife.

"Anyway," said Amy, "we know how much you wanted to work at the inn, and I know that we never really talked about it, but *of course* there's a spot for you. If you want to work a few hours at the front desk, or if you want to play concierge... anything you want!"

"Thank you," I said, nodding my head. "I appreciate that. And a few weeks ago, I'd have said yes in a heartbeat. A few weeks ago, all I wanted was to fill my days with working at the store, or the inn, or the mini mart. But now..." I trailed off. "Is, um, is Riley home yet, do you know?"

"I don't think so," said Amy, studying my face. "But he left this morning, so he should be here in a few hours. He seemed sort of out of it all week. Like, his mind was elsewhere. I didn't even see him playing Pokémon Go. Did you?" She looked at her husband.

"Nope," said Kit, shaking his head. "He seemed sort of depressed."

"He didn't even try to plan my funeral," added Tom. "That kid was definitely not himself. Drugs, maybe."

"Weird," I said, my mind racing. Riley hadn't been playing Pokémon Go? His most favorite thing in the world? In an instant, that seemingly silly piece of information swept away any last doubts about his feelings for me. They were real. And he'd missed me.

* * *

IT WAS quiet at my house.

My family had all gone back home, none of them even asking for a penny before they left. Audrey actually *hugged* me, and then —in a very Buzz from *Home Alone* sort of moment—said that it was cool, what I'd done for all those people. Randy said he understood now why I liked to waste my money on that sort of thing. They both offered to come back next year to help out again.

Now, it was dark outside, and I was stretched out on the couch, not really paying attention to the episode of *Supernatural* on the screen. Pixie was by my side and my phone was in my hand. I'd finally come up with the words to text to Riley. Wherever he was.

I miss you. Come home.

My hands were shaking as I hit send. I immediately received an "I'm Driving with Do Not Disturb Turned On" message in return. So, he was on the road; that was good news. I waited a bit longer, but by eleven o'clock I'd given up. He must have driven straight back to his apartment. Maybe he'd never even seen my text. Maybe I'd been wrong about everything.

I turned off the television and was heading upstairs, when the doorbell rang. I froze on the bottom step, Pixie barking at the door. At this hour, there were only a few possibilities of who might be out there. I grabbed the baseball bat that I kept next to the refrigerator, and looked through the peephole. My stomach dissolved into butterflies as I wrenched open the door.

Riley held his phone in the air, my message visible on the screen. "I thought maybe I should reply to this in person."

I dropped the baseball bat with a thud, stepped forward, and threw my arms around his neck. He slipped his arms around my waist, and we stood there like that for a while, the cold air streaming through the open door.

"I'm sorry I took off like that," he said. "And I'm sorry it took me so long to get back. Traffic."

I just nodded into his shoulder.

"Were you planning to hit me with that bat?"

I laughed and took a step back, pulling him into the house and closing the door behind us. "I wasn't going to hit you."

"Good," he said, pushing a piece of hair off my forehead.

"Because I missed you, too." His dark eyes locked onto mine, making my knees go weak.

"I'm coming with you," I said, staring right back at him. I was so glad he was home. "I've decided."

"Yeah?" he asked, a small smile forming on his lips.

I nodded. "We go together, we come home together." I stuck out my hand. "Deal?"

He took my hand, slowly shaking it up and down while keeping his eyes on my face. Then he pulled me closer and lowered his head, his lips inches from my own. "Best deal I ever made, Moneybags."

With his lips pressed warmly against mine, and Pixie running circles around our feet, that final weight lifted from my chest. I let out a yelp of surprise as he scooped me up and carried me into the living room. He flopped down on the couch, leaning back against the pillows, holding me on his lap.

"I was worried when I heard you hadn't been playing Pokémon Go," I said, playing with the zipper on his sweatshirt.

"I just wasn't feeling it," he said, gently kissing the back of my hand, sending shivers down my spine. "I'm not sure why...but I'm suddenly feeling much better."

I smiled. "You realize we're about to travel around the *world* playing that game, right? I don't know if you're taking it seriously enough. We've got some catching up to do."

"Yes, we do," he said, swiftly flipping me onto my back. "Tomorrow."

"Tomorrow." I smiled.

I looked up into his eyes, my fingers tangled in his hair, so thankful for everything I'd been given and everything yet to come.

Tomorrow was going to be great.

NEXT THANKSGIVING

"*I*'m just so excited about the babies!" I said, scooping mashed potatoes onto my plate before passing the bowl along to Riley. "I have so many ideas! Xenophilius and Luna—"

"Xeno *what?*" asked Amy.

"Opal and Pearl," I continued.

"Which one of those would be the boy?" asked Kit, glancing around the table.

"Ooh, or Titania and Oberon!" I said, ignoring both of their comments. "From *A Midsummer Night's Dream,* you know? King and queen of the fairies! What could be sweeter?"

I looked across the table at Kit and Amy, whose faces had both frozen into semi-horrified half-smiles.

"I am *not* naming my son Oberon," said Kit, shaking his head. "No way."

"Yeah, sorry, Josie," said Amy. "Oberon's just a little too close to Orion." She shuddered at the name of her ex. I loved that they thought I was serious.

There were twenty of us for Thanksgiving this year. Me, Mom,

Dad, Granny, Riley, Kit, Amy, Tom, Maggie, Amy's parents, Meg and her family, Uncle Burt, Aunt Carla, Audrey, and Randy. Half of us had hosted the free community dinner earlier in the day—which seemed to be turning into an Autumnboro tradition—and now the whole lovely gang was at my house, seated at two long, candlelit tables in front of the windows overlooking the Pemigewasset.

It's only been a month since Riley and I returned from Bora Bora (our ocean hut was just as amazing as everybody said it would be), and since Kit and Amy announced that they were having twins. Twins! I'd already ordered them so many things from QVC, they had *no* idea.

Riley and I have done a lot of traveling this past year. The Pokémon Go trip was just the start of it, and what a whirlwind adventure that had been. For three weeks, we hopped from Japan to China to Spain, and then on to France and Italy—my heart and soul filling up with new experiences, new people, new food. And while a good part of our trip was spent staring at our phones and playing that addictive little game, that wasn't nearly the whole of it. We ziplined off the Eiffel Tower and went clubbing in Ibiza; we drove go-karts around the streets of Tokyo and looked up at the Tian Tan Buddha; we saw the Mona Lisa, and the Colosseum, and I believe it was on our second to last night in Venice—when Riley nearly dropped his phone off the gondola and into the canal—that I realized my crush was creeping dangerously close to love. Only, it hadn't felt very dangerous at all. Just safe, and calm, and happy.

As promised, we left on our trip together, and we returned home to Autumnboro together. We haven't been apart since.

While we were away, Mom and Dad offered to come up to watch the store. As it turned out, they enjoyed their time in Autumnboro so much that they put their house in Massachusetts on the market, and bought one two miles from mine. Dad comes by the store all the time now—sometimes to talk to me, but usually to hang out with Tom and Moose, who formed an unofficial woodworking club by the fireplace.

Lee started college this fall at Plymouth State, so Dad's also been enjoying looking over his coursework, giving him pointers on note-taking, and whatever other things retired teachers are into.

Upon returning home from Pennsylvania last Thanksgiving, Maggie finally decided it was time to retire for good, which left Artie Goldwyn in need of a part-time secretary. Mom—for all the times she asked me *why* I wanted to work when I could just relax —scooped up the job in a heartbeat. I smiled at her, down at the end of the table, sipping her wine and talking animatedly to Dad. I didn't even think she'd gone for any pre-Thanksgiving Botox this year.

Granny was sitting beside her, smiling at Riley, which she tended to do a *lot.* Not that I could blame her. He looked so handsome in the gray and black cardigan I'd picked out for him (the fact that I'd ordered a matching one for Pixie was a surprise I was saving for after dinner). Riley caught me staring and smiled back.

"Did you order enough pies this year?" asked Uncle Burt, loosening his pants. "Because last year I don't think there were enough pies!" He let out a loud guffaw. I was just thankful he seemed to have given up the spaceship to Mars joke.

"There are plenty of pies, Uncle Burt," I said, standing up and clearing away some plates. "I'll start taking them out."

"I'm going to run to the bathroom," said Riley, a bit too loudly. He stood, bumping the table with his legs, making everybody's drinks slosh up the sides of their glasses.

"Um, okay," I said, looking at him, my eyebrows raised. "Thanks for the info."

"I'll help you in the kitchen after I'm done," he said, in a strange robot voice that I'd never heard before.

"Great." I patted him on the back as he left the room. Why was he acting so weird? So nervous? It was almost like the way he *used* to act around me.

I was in the kitchen, scraping turkey and stuffing into the trash, when a noise by the sink made me look up. It was Riley, leaning against the counter and watching me. His eyes kept flicking from me to the refrigerator. Me to the refrigerator.

"You okay?" I asked. Maybe he was just really jonesing for some of that pie.

"Yeah. Of, course. Why wouldn't I be?"

He pulled out his phone and started tapping at the screen, which made things feel slightly more normal. I put the plates into the sink and opened the refrigerator. I took out two pie boxes, placed them on the counter, then went back into the fridge for more. It was after I had lifted the third box that I saw it—the large plastic coffee cup with the dome lid, way at the back of the shelf. It was filled with the rich, amber color of a Maple Sugar Crush, and on the cup, written in black Sharpie, were two words:

Marry Me?

BENEATH THE TWO words was drawn a simple, scribbled heart. The pie box dropped from my hands, hitting the floor with a thud and a splat, which drew the attention of everybody still seated at the tables.

"Are you okay?" somebody called out—my sister, I think—but I just continued staring into the refrigerator, one hand going to my mouth.

"I hope that wasn't the pecan!" shouted Uncle Burt.

"More like pe-can't!" That was Randy. Still, I didn't move.

I heard more murmuring from the tables, and the sound of chairs scooting back, and people walking over to investigate. In slow motion, my hands shaking, I pulled out the coffee cup and turned to look for Riley. He'd put his phone away and was down on one knee in the middle of my kitchen. He had a ring box in one hand, and Pixie beside him. She was already dressed in her gray and black sweater.

"How did you—" I pointed dumbly at Pixie. Riley down on one knee was too much to process at the moment. But Pixie in her sweater…we could start there.

"Because I know you, Moneybags," said Riley. "I knew that if you'd bought *me* a sweater, you must've bought Pixie one to match." He put one hand to the side of his mouth. "And because Granny told me it was hidden in the spare bedroom."

I laughed and swiped at my eyes that had been rapidly filling with tears. "Well, you two look adorable. It's everything I dreamed it would be. It's perfect."

"Yeah?"

"Yeah." My eyes shifted to the ring box, then back to Riley, silently urging him on. "Well, almost."

I could tell that he was nervous. Proposing was no easy business, never mind doing it in front of my entire family. I'd make this easy on him.

"What do you say, Josephine?" The way he said my name sent shivers down my spine. "Will you marry me?"

"Yes!" I nodded. "Yes. Of course, I'll marry you."

I put the cup down on the counter and wrapped my arms around his neck. Uncle Burt wolf-whistled. Pixie barked and pawed at our legs, as if she knew exactly what was going on. As if she knew that this house would soon be filled with double the love and double the belly rubs.

"I know it's not champagne," said Riley, after we'd finally broken apart. He was looking at the Maple Sugar Crush on the counter. "But, should we split it?"

"I'd love some."

I waited while he carefully poured the somewhat melted

drink between two champagne flutes. We clinked glasses and each took a sip. The coffee was rich and sweet and reminded me of summer. I stood on my toes and kissed him on the cheek.

"I love you," I said, nuzzling into his neck.

"I love you, too." His lips pressed against my forehead, one arm around my waist. I closed my eyes.

Somehow, I'd gone and hit the lottery twice. The first time was nothing but pure luck. Just a random bunch of numbers on a slip of paper. That one, I'm sharing with the world, one good deed at a time.

But the second time? The time that this amazing person ended up in my life, one arm wrapped around my waist, telling me that he loves me? I'm sorry to say, but that one's all mine. I'd really like to share, but he's one of a kind. Life is so much sweeter now, with Riley by my side.

Sweeter than maple sugar.

The End

OTHER BOOKS BY BETH LABONTE

The Summer Series:

Summer at Sea

Summer at Sunset

Summer Baby

Holiday Sweet Romance:

Love Notes in Reindeer Falls

Autumnboro Sweet Romance:

Pumpkin Everything (Book 1)

Maple Sugar Crush (Book 2)

More:

Down, Then Up: A Novella

You can also find Beth here:

Facebook

www.bethlabonte.com

Printed in Great Britain
by Amazon